THE IRANICAN DREAM

Siamack Baniameri

"The Iranican Dream," by Siamack Baniameri. ISBN 1-58939-677-4.

Published 2005 by Virtualbookworm.com Publishing Inc., P.O. Box 9949, College Station, TX 77842, US.

Cover licensed by Stockbyte.

Manufactured in the United States of America.

1. It Sucks Being Me

BEING A MIDDLE EASTERN-AMERICAN MAN nowadays is as hard as a stash of beef jerky sitting on top of a pickup truck's dashboard in the Arizona summer heat. You sure grow thick skin. But being a Middle Eastern single parent in America and raising two teenagers is by far the armpit of all human sufferings.

It's not easy parenting two punk teenagers who think they know it all and believe their father is the retarded member of the household. My smart-ass kids look down on me as if I just arrived in the country on a camel, and every time I open my mouth to say something, they correct my grammar or laugh at my accent. They treat me as though I lived in the caves of Afghanistan before coming to America. How can I effectively perform my parental chores in a situation like this? I'm dying here.

I tell my kids, "You think I speak funny? Why don't you try speaking my native language, and let's hear how you sound, you bastards."

From day one I realized that America is all about challenges. The challenge of parenthood, the challenge of balancing home and career, the challenge of dating, the challenge of staying fit, the challenge of relationships—the list goes on and on.

Now, you want challenge? Live my life: come to America from the Middle East; learn a new language, new customs, new lifestyle; raise two teenagers from hell by yourself; constantly plot to sabotage your ex-wife's relationships; go into hiding to avoid your crazy family and friends; get strip-searched every time you pass through airport security; shave your five o'clock shadow three times a day so you don't accidentally look like one of those pictures of the FBI's ten most wanted terrorists; and constantly wonder if the Department of Homeland Security has planted a camera in your shower.

That's challenge, folks, and I am not kidding you. Now, the most challenging part of being a Middle Eastern man in the United States is constantly having to explain to the average Joe where you've come from.

"So, where are you from again?"

"I'm from Iran."

"Which state is that?"

"It's a country, not a state."

"Oh, yeah. Mexico?"

"No, it's in the Middle East."

"Oh, yeah, you guys shouldn't have done the nine-eleven thing, man. That was not cool."

"Iran had nothing to do with nine-eleven."

"Yeah, right. But we sure kicked your asses, huh?"

"That's Iraq, a different country."

"Yeah, right. So where is your buddy, Osama?"

"If I knew where the bastard was, I would've turned him in and collected the twenty-five-million-dollar reward."

"I've been overseas myself, you know. I went to Nogales, Mexico, for spring break once. I got so wasted, I was, like, sick for two weeks."

"Nice."

"Hey, man, about that twenty-five million dollars? Like, if I go to the Middle East and find Osama, do I, like, get the whole reward?"

"I guess."

"So, like, where is he?"

"I don't know. He was last spotted near downtown. Take 202 west and exit at Broadway. That's a good place to start."

"Thanks, man. I don't care what they say about you Mexicans; but you're all right in my book."

"Middle Eastern, not Mexican."

"Yeah, whatever."

Now, I feel that my kids are ashamed of my accent, and they avoid telling their friends the truth about their father's background. I guess they are influenced by the constant images of rock-throwing, car-burning, gun-slinging Middle Eastern men on television. And when was the last time you saw a Hollywood movie with a Middle Eastern hero? Let's see, Clint Eastwood is not Middle Eastern, neither is Bruce Willis, Arnold, Van Damme, or Brad Pitt.

Hollywood movies portray Middle Eastern men as second-class losers or sidekick terrorists with constantly bad hairdos. Looks like the Native Americans and the African-Americans have been replaced by us.

I don't blame my kids for not acknowledging their father's roots. Would you want to point at a terrorist getting shot by Bruce Willis in a movie and say to your friends, "Hey, that dude looks just like my dad."

Every time my kids have friends over, they introduce me as Abdul, the rug cleaner, or Hassan, the Middle Eastern plumber. It sucks having your own kids disown you like that. But it's okay because I have my own ways of getting even with them.

For example: I walk up to my daughter's guy friends and say, "Hi, I'm her dad, and I'm from the Middle East. If you ever, ever, ever touch her, I will blow up your house. Have a nice day and come again."

You should see the look on the poor kid's face. Before you can count to three, the kid runs out of the house screaming for help, and my daughter cries, "Thanks, Dad. My social life stinks because of you."

"You're welcome, pumpkin."

Or when my son brings a female classmate home to study in his room (yeah, I'm sure they're studying), I burst into the room, pull up my shirt, expose my hairy back, and say, "Son, it's time for our weekly back-shaving party. You shave my back, I shave yours."

But my kids have developed good lies to counter my attacks.

"Hey, your dad talks funny."

"Yeah, my dad is really from Knox County, Texas, and he had a horrifying accident when he was a kid. Half of his tongue was cut off when his bicycle hit his uncle's pickup truck in a head-on collision."

One thing I can't stand is hearing grownups whining about their childhood.

The other day, this guy at work was telling me how bad he had it when he was a kid. Non-stop popularity contests in high school, playing with outdated video games while all the other kids played with the latest and the greatest games, being dragged by his parents from piano lessons to arts and crafts, being pressured by his folks to practice sports that he didn't care much about, being grounded for days for smoking pot, blah, blah, blah. I asked the chum to stop for a second so I could get my violin. What a bunch of crap.

Kids in America have it easy. American parents are so patient and thoughtful when it comes to raising their kids. They spend millions of dollars every year buying books by renowned psychologists that teach them how to raise their children in peaceful and healthy surroundings. American parents go out of their way to make sure their children are brought up to realize their highest potential. Isn't that precious?

"Little Johnny should be raised by applying reasoning in a nonviolent environment where we can teach him valuable lessons that will later inform his behavior towards others."

Now this one is my favorite: "Little Johnny is so much more receptive to criticism when we reason with him in a non-threatening voice and in a calm manner."

When kids get in trouble, their parents sit them down at the kitchen table and reason with them, "Little Johnny, you should have never called your mom a bitch. That is no way to speak to grownups."

"But she is a bitch. She didn't buy me ice cream. I want ice cream. Ice cream."

"Son, I understand that your mother can be difficult sometimes, but that gives you no right to insult her. Now, go kiss

Mommy and apologize. Okay, you're a good boy."

When I was growing up in Iran, our parents never talked to us like that. Not even once. Not even a word or sentence that remotely resembled that.

Growing up in Iran, you learn one thing quickly: grownups do not take crap from kids. End of story. If I had ever called my mom "bitch," all hell would have broken loose, and my father would have rushed into the room with a belt in one hand and a dagger in the other. You would have seen murder in his eyes, and his face would have been red, as if he were about to explode.

"Did you call your mother a 'bitch'? Huh? Did you? Nobody in this house calls your mother a bitch except me, you son of a bitch. I'll whip your ass first then I'll cut you up into small pieces and feed you to stray dogs. And I'll donate your organs to the Red Cross and buy your brothers and sisters new bicycles with the money."

Years of eating shish kabob and basmati rice had taken its toll on my dad. His big, fat body slowed down his reflexes and limited his movements. That gave me an extra few seconds to get out of his way. If I had stayed in the room, my father would have lashed my ass like Zorro. If I managed to get out of the room, he would fling the dagger like a Ringling Brothers circus act.

If by some miracle, I managed to dodge the dagger, I would immediately run into my mother, who was waiting for me in the hallway with a shovel.

"So you called me a 'bitch?' Huh? Did you? Only your father can call me a bitch in this house, you son of a bitch. I'm going to dig a grave with this shovel and dump your body in there."

"Oh, yeah? What you gonna say to my friends when they ask for me?" I would reply.

"I tell 'em you ran away."

"Shit."

I knew if I stayed there, my mother would do some serious damage with that shovel. So I would fake left, fake right, and get out of her way like a bat out of hell. And just when I thought I was home free, I would find my eighty-five-year-old grandma in the yard, waiting for me with a broomstick in her hands. Like a crazy ninja, granny would do a one-and-a-half somersault followed by two back flips and shatter the broomstick right on my head.

In my family, beating kids was a customary habit that had been passed on from one generation to another. The family truly believed in disciplining lads by beating the crap out of them. My family was so good at punishing their kids that friends and neighbors would often invite them to hold seminars in the art of "kicking lads to a better future."

This was a group activity. A national sport. Everybody would participate. Other family members and neighbors were all welcome to get in on the action:

"Hey, what's going on over there?"

"We are punishing our son. Come on in, there is still plenty of room."

"All right, hey, I got some guests over at my house. Can I call them to join us?"

"Sure. The more the merrier."

Kids here have it good. Trust me on that. When I was a kid, sometimes my mom would punish me for no apparent reason. I'm doing my homework, and then WHAM, my mom would hit me in the head with a pan.

"What the hell was that for?"

"Your punishment for today just in case you do something wrong and we miss it."

"What a bitch."

"What did you call me?"

"Oh, no."

It was even worse at school. I had a math teacher who was very good at throwing objects from his desk. You said something he didn't like, and the stapler would fly and hit you in the nose. You gave a wrong answer to a math question, and the eraser would whack you in the eye at sixty miles per hour.

The music teacher had developed his own beating techniques, which were very effective. He would fake with his right hand and smack you in the face with his left. You wouldn't know what hit you. He would move down and throw an uppercut with such lightning speed that you could see it only by watching the sports highlights in slow motion on TV. The man knew his stuff.

The geography teacher walked around the classroom with a long wooden stick. He would let it soak in water before the class started. That would make the lashes hurt more and last longer. He would point at a country on a map hanging on the wall and ask students to name the capital of that country. If you gave him a wrong answer, he would whip you with his wet stick until it broke. Then he would leave the classroom and return with a fresh batch.

For some reason, I always ended up with countries that one never hears about. Like, who knows the capital of Lesotho or Mauritius? I didn't even know those countries existed.

That sucked bad because if you said something to your parents about the beating you got at school, they would pull out their own tools and beat the booboo out of you just for getting in trouble at school. It was all very complicated.

Being a parent in the United States is a drag because I can't beat up my own kids the way I'd like to. You have no idea how many times I've been arrested for beating the crap out of my teenagers. A little bruise here or there, and I get picked up by the cops. What's up with that?

"Sir, have you been beating your kids?"

"Officer, spend just two hours with them, and you'll do the same."

The other day my fourteen-year-old son walks into the house with his filthy shoes on, drops his backpack on the floor, walks to the fridge, drinks milk from the carton, leaves the fridge door open, doesn't say hi to anyone, goes to his room, slams the door shut, and yells, "Life sucks."

His pants are falling off, and you can clearly see his butt crack. He's wearing a T-shirt that says "blow me" and his hair looks like Saddam Hussein's did when he was pulled out of the spider hole. The kid is getting all F's at school and spends all his waking hours playing with his Xbox.

"How can life suck?" I asked. "You don't work, you don't study. You don't pay for rent, electricity, water, car, clothes, shoes, or anything at all. You don't do your own laundry, clean the house, or wash the dishes. You have no responsibilities; how in the world can life suck?"

He rushes out of his room and yells, "Life sucks 'cause I ain't got the new Tommy Hilfiger, man."

"Tommy who?"

"Dad, you don't know Jack."

"Jack who?"

"Dad, it's impossible to have a normal conversation with you. Go back to Iran."

Last year I told my kids that it was time to call on the homeland. I told them that we were going to Iran to visit the family, and they were going to learn about their father's culture and customs. The plan was to get them to Iran for two weeks and then beat the shit out of them in a free and friendly environment where no one prosecutes you for disciplining your children, and people are always ready to join in and give you a hand.

I was hoping to employ my family's expertise in disciplining kids, utilizing the latest in the art of teenager-ass-whipping.

"Hey, Ma, bringing the kids over to the old country for some serious ass-whipping."

"You are?" my mom said. "I can't wait to see my grandchildren."

"Mom, this is strictly business. I want you to beat manners, discipline, and respect into these kids."

"No problem, honey. Bring them over, and I'll get the neighbors."

This was great, I was reaching out for help and as always, the family was there for me.

Well, my kids are too smart for their own good. They told me that they won't leave the protection of the United States of America until they are bigger than me. "Nice try, Dad."

I went to their teacher the other day to bring up issues that needed to be addressed. I wanted to consult with the teacher and find out if there are any alternatives to disciplining kids other than five rounds of full-contact kickboxing. The teacher looked awful. She pulled me aside and said, "Are you kidding me? You have no idea how many times a day I want to take these kids' heads off and feed them to vultures. Bunch of little monsters feeding off their parents' ignorance and egos, making my life a living hell. If I could just get ten minutes with each of those kids in a small unmonitored room, I would teach them a lesson they wouldn't forget."

I was delighted to see the teacher as irritated and frustrated as I was when it came to disciplining and modifying the teenagers' behavior. I felt that the teacher and I had something in common: we both wanted to give all teenagers a good beating. There was no question that the teacher and I had some sort of a spiritual connection, and I would have asked her out if she hadn't looked so much like Danny DeVito in drag.

Don't get me wrong. I'll be the first to admit that I have completely failed as a parent and a husband. You probably think that I'm the psycho dad, and I'm totally out of my mind. "Oh, my God. This Middle Eastern guy wants to beat his kids."

I'm sorry you feel that way, but I believe that kids, like all other intelligent creatures, respond better to your commands if they fear you. When I was a kid and my dad told me to do something, I would jump out of my seat like a loaded spring and get on with it. I did it not because I was a good kid; I did it because he scared the shit out of me.

But this interaction with the teacher gave me a great idea. I'm going to collect enough signatures to pass a law that would allow parents of all teenagers across the U.S. to join their kids once a week in the schoolyard and beat the bazooka out of them for one hour.

Teenaged kids will be running around chased by parents armed with baseball bats. No discrimination whatsoever. All kids will get it: good, bad, nasty. We'd beat them all.

This could be a family affair. A paid holiday. I'll bring my dad, mom, and grandma to participate. I'll have my dad accompany me with his belt and dagger, mom will stay behind to cover our backs and grandma will cover the exit just in case some of those spoiled brats get away.

This will be a fun day for all parents, and I guarantee that your kids will behave better than ever, and they won't disrespect, challenge, or question your authority again. Oh, don't forget to bring the neighbors.

2. My Love Life Sucks

I'M NOT THE SHARPEST KNIFE IN THE KITCHEN when it comes to dating women. I'm rough around the edges, and I don't play well with others. My style is raw. I see what I like, and—BOOM—I go for the throat. The way I see it, she'll either give in to my manly charms, or she'll call the cops (mostly the case).

Ever since the wife left me, I've come to grips with certain realities in life. For example: having two teenage kids does not help your chances of dating women. Having two kids and being Middle Eastern reduces your chances of getting a decent date by another fifty percent. Having two kids, being Middle Eastern, and having a bad attitude makes finding dates close to impossible.

My ideal date would be a Middle Eastern-American female in her mid-twenties with big breasts. It's cultural compatibility that I'm after, and big breasts don't hurt either. But at this point I'm open to dating anything that has a tiny resemblance to the female of any species. As a matter fact, I date any woman that breathes. Hey, I'm honest.

My aggressive style doesn't sit well with some women. Most women like guys who are—how can I put it in gentle terms—pussy-whipped. They like to keep their man on a short leash. They like guys who are kind, gentle, affectionate, intelligent, understanding, compromising, passionate, spiritual, modest, funny, metrosexual, and, of course, most important, loaded with cash. Hey, there is nothing wrong with wanting it all. If you can ever find a man like that, more power to you, sister. Make sure you ride him like a pony and milk him like a cow.

Meeting quality women in the U.S. is definitely hard work. Back in the Middle East, meeting women is easy. The man doesn't have to do a thing. We men rely on a network of overly enthusiastic female family members who pick and choose our mates for us. It's kind of like an unofficial family pimping service. The radar is constantly searching and seeking quality targets.

If you're a lazy man like me, you don't do a damn thing. You sit down, relax, and let the system work for you. They line up all kinds of beautiful and intelligent women, and you get to choose the one or two or three that suit your style. How much easier can it get?

Another good thing about the system is that you don't have to take your newly selected companion out to dinner or dancing, which is great for your pocket if you're cheap like me. You basically check her out, make sure all the pieces are in the right place, and voila. You say the word, and she is your future wife. Baddabing, baddaboom. The woman's family even pays for the wedding. Is this cool or what?

And the best part of this so-called arranged marriage is the limited time you spend with her before you're married. That way she will never truly get to know you, and she won't have a clue as to what kind of selfish idiot you really are. That always helps.

But here in the U.S. you actually have to work for love. You have to go out there and find a woman, then you have to meet several times in different locations, then you have to put on a good show and behave like a gentleman to prove to her what a great catch you are. And then you have to slowly bring her into your life. Of course, you hope she is in love with you by the time she gets to know the real you and realizes how screwed up your life is. Now that takes a lot of planning, and I have no patience for that.

I was at a job interview the other night. Well, it was really a date, but it felt like a job interview. You see, my date was in her late thirties. Ain't nothing wrong with that except her biological clock was ticking, and I'm NOT talking "tick, tick," it was more like "BANG, BANG." You could hear it from a mile away.

Don't get me wrong. I've nothing against older women, but I must think of my future. My kids are going to leave and go on their own in another two or three years, and I'll be all alone. I'm not exactly young, either. At my age, I should have a solid retirement plan in place. So, I figure, I should find a younger woman who will have the energy and the enthusiasm to take care of me after my first heart attack which—judging by my high cholesterol—should happen any day now. Okay, I'm a pig.

Naturally, my date was in the market to find her cash cow. Aren't we all? It's just that the cow sitting across the table happened to be me. She was all business, no messing around on her part, a real no-nonsense Middle Eastern lady. Being older, I guess she didn't have much time to waste. She kind of reminded me of me: a woman who knows what she wants but doesn't have the time or stamina to go look for it. It's sad if you think about it.

Single older women are unique in a sense that they're quite capable of spotting a bullshitter from a mile away. They're very accomplished in controlling their emotions and hormones at times when important decisions are made. They also have this distinctive ability to manipulate without a flinch, which makes them dangerous and unpredictable. That's why single older women should be handled by the most experienced men, and younger men should never explore that territory unless they don't mind being eaten alive.

"I'm going to ask you three questions," she said. "These questions will allow me to better understand what kind of a man you are and what kind of a future I can have with you."

"Excuse me, come again?"

She went on without hesitation, "I believe a woman should constantly improve her image. Since Iranian men are old-fashioned, how do you feel about my getting plastic surgery?"

"Well, it's okay with me as long as the surgery increases the size of certain body parts and enables you to audition for Baywatch."

"I'm not talking breast implants. I'm talking about a nose job," she said.

"I'm not so sure about that. Think of it this way. You get the breast implants, and no one will look at your face anymore. So you kill two birds with one stone."

She looked at me with resentment for a moment. It was one of those looks that women give you when they're not sure whether to smack you or kick you in the balls. She ground her teeth in disgust and continued, "I am a successful career woman. Since Iranian men are overly jealous, how would it make you feel if I went on an overnight business trip with my boss?"

I'm getting jealous already, and I don't even know her. But I come up with a clever answer.

"Whatever. Can we talk more about that breast-implant surgery?"

"I take these questions very seriously. Please be careful about your answers," she said. This woman was beginning to scare me. She started to remind me of my math teacher back home. I was waiting for her to throw a plate at me.

"Okay, take it easy. I'm just having fun," I replied

"Well, don't have fun at my expense."

"Okay, sorry."

"Last question and last chance to redeem yourself," she barked. "If you, your mom, and I are trapped on a deserted island, and we have food for only two people, who would you chose to share the food with? Me or your mom?"

You don't mess with an Iranian man's mom. That's forbidden territory. It's sacred, and it will remain that way forever. So I gave her an answer that set the record straight, "That would all depend on whether you got those breast implants or not."

"Listen, you hairy asshole. I have no time to waste on you. I'm going to give you one more chance. You screw this up, and I'm out of here."

"Fine."

She looked deep into my eyes and said in a threatening voice, "I hate men that don't make the effort to satisfy me in bed. Since Iranian men are lazy in bed, how far would you go to satisfy me?"

I was surprised to hear that! How did she know I was lazy in bed? Had she talked to my ex-wife? Does she work for the Department of Homeland Security?

"Well, between me being trapped on a deserted island and you being on a business trip with your boss, I don't think we should worry about that," I replied.

I felt a cold sensation of iced tea being splashed on my head. She got up and walked away in decisive strides. She stopped and yelled from across the room, "Just to let you know, I am getting breast implants next week."

I got down on my knees and yelled back, "What? Wait, ask one more question; I'll do better. Come back here. I love you, don't go . . . please, somebody, stop her."

My kids are supportive of my dating activities. I suspect they just want me out of the house for a few hours so they can have friends over. They always encourage me to meet a nice lady and marry her. I guess they want a clean house and decent warm food for a change.

My worst dating experience came a few years ago when I was set up by a friend to meet an Iranian-American lady.

Yes, it was a blind date. Not exactly my style, but I figured what the heck? Things hadn't been going my way. I was getting older. My self-esteem was low. The front of my hair was getting closer to the back of my neck, my belly was pushing down on my belt, and there was hair growing on parts of my body that would even make a monkey laugh.

"So, is she good looking?" I asked the friend who was arranging the whole event.

"That all depends on your definition of good looking."

"Well, let me rephrase the question. Does she have more hair on her face than I do?"

"Yeah, but it's softer than yours."

Anyhow, women were not exactly lined up at my door. I couldn't even remember the last time I had gone on a date.

"So how did you describe me to her?" I asked my friend.

"Oh, you know. I told her you have a great personality."

"Thanks. Now she thinks I am ugly."

"You are ugly," my friend said, laughing.

All right, the man was honest. But I was not going to allow my physical imperfections to have a negative effect on my personality. I was determined to show this woman what a great, fun-loving, and smart guy I am. That's right, I'm The Man.

Well, deep inside, I know that I don't have much of a personality. Combine that with lack of funds and ambition and add two punk teenaged kids to the package, and you might as well sit home and lick that ice cream bucket for the rest of your life. I'm talking a lot pressure to overcome here. God, my life sucks!

We were meeting in a coffee shop at the corner of Third and Broadway. It's a New Yorker thing to do. I was nervous. What if she's smart and beautiful? What if she expects me to recite Khayyam? What if she talks politics? Should I speak Farsi or English? What if she's The One?

I intentionally got there early. I needed to find a perfect spot where I could have my back against the wall. I didn't want her to accidentally catch a glimpse at my bald spots. (Okay, I'm insecure; so shoot me.) As I was adjusting the strategic location of my chair and looking around for the waitress, all of a sudden, a little guy sat down on the chair in front of me.

"Excuse me, sir, but this chair is taken. I'm expecting someone," I barked.

"I'm not a SIR, you ignorant Iranian man," he said.

I looked closer. What the hell...? It's not a guy. It's a woman, and it's my date. A little, bleached-blond woman with a very short haircut, wearing a long white T-shirt, baggy jeans and sneakers. I have a date with Slim Shady.

"I don't do blind dates," she said. "I'm only here because I owe Sammy [my pal] a favor. And I'm not your typical Iranian woman. I'm an assistant director of a successful off-Broadway show. I'm very much a New Yorker. I don't take shit from no one, especially from chauvinist Iranian men who think women belong in the kitchen. I refuse to become a second-class citizen. I find Iranian men incapable of expressing themselves emotionally and artistically. I find Iranian men a bunch of single-minded hooligans who are like puppets controlled by their mothers. I find that extremely revolting. I'm an artist. I contribute to the beautification of minds."

I needed a minute to take in all that information and analyze the situation. Why is she so mad already? It usually takes two dates before women start yelling at me. And how did she know I'm a chauvinist who is controlled by his mom? Had she been talking to my ex-wife? Did she work for the Department of Homeland Security?

"Uh, would you like some coffee?" I asked.

"No, I buy my own coffee. I don't want you to pay for my coffee. You probably think I'm a poor and helpless Iranian woman who needs protection. You're probably going to stand up on the table and start banging on your hairy chest like Tarzan. I don't need you. I don't need anybody."

Holy cow! I'm sitting in front of the most militant Iranian-American feminist in New York City. I'm convinced now that God is playing a bad joke on me. What crimes could I have possibly committed to deserve this? This is a nightmare. I was wondering if my friend was having fun with this one. That son of a bitch probably set me up with her to get even for my borrowing all that money and never repaying him. "Sooo, what's the name of the Broadway show you're directing?" I said.

"I'm not a director. I'm an assistant director of an off-Broadway show. You are a typical Iranian man. You have no listening skills. You have no concentration when it comes to women's careers. If I were talking about football or stupid wrestling, you would have been all over that, but no, God forbid I talk about my career, dreams and aspirations. You make me sick."

I couldn't get a break from this woman. I crashed and burned on every word that came out of my mouth. This was the ultimate test of my patience, of which I had none, and I was going to fail this test miserably.

I took a deep breath and started thinking hard to come up with a subject to talk about that wouldn't offend her.

"So, have you seen a good movie lately? I hear The Matrix is pretty good," I said.

"I don't watch stupid Hollywood movies. I watch foreign movies and theater, which is something you Iranian men have never heard of."

Okay, next subject.

"And by the way," she went on, "I really don't care what you do for a living. I find Iranian men conservative and boring when it comes to choosing a profession. Why is it that you never meet an Iranian stuntman, skydiving instructor, river guide, or model? Why do they have to always pick these boring professions like engineering, selling cars, or dentistry?"

"Well, you gotta make good money to buy earplugs," I replied.

"Excuse YOU? Are you suggesting that I talk too much, you miserable old man?"

"Sorry, I wasn't expecting to talk about money on the first date," I exclaimed.

"This is not a date—okay? And money is all you Iranian men think about. You have to make the money so you can drive your stupid BMWs around and show off with loud techno music blasting out of your cars. It's all about money for you guys. You're all materialistic."

I'm getting pissed off now. That's it. She insulted me and my mom and I can tolerate that. But nobody, and I mean nobody, insults my BMW. Okay, let me explain this one more time: there are two things that are off limits when it comes to an Iranian man. One is his mother, and the other is his German car.

"Listen, lady, will you get off my back? You may be right. Maybe I'm chauvinist, materialistic and insensitive. Maybe I'm controlled by my mother. Maybe I don't have listening skills and can't concentrate for more than five seconds. But at least this is the way I have always been. At least I didn't lose my identity and change into a rude and selfish New Yorker with an attitude. At least I didn't bleach my hair and dress like a boy rap star. No, YOU make me sick."

I'm not exactly sure what in the world I was talking about, but that's the best I could do under pressure.

I stood up, picked up my jacket like a tough guy, and walked away. As I was passing her, I heard her say, "So, are you gonna call me?"

Yeah, when camels fly.

I told my friends that I had given up on dating. There was no point. I was sure that there was no one out there that was suitable for me. This was not worth the humiliation and embarrassment that I felt every time I returned home from a date.

My cousin, Reza, suggested that I should meet women online. He said that he has been corresponding with number of breathtaking women on the Internet, and he was having the time of his life. Even though I did not trust Reza's judgment, I figured why not. I had nothing to lose.

Reza gave me the URL of a chat room that he had joined and expressed his total satisfaction with the quality of the women he had met so far. He said that the women in the chat room were frank, open-minded and sexy. He said that some women in the chat room might be overly aggressive, but I was okay with that.

I've never been crazy about the idea of meeting the opposite sex on the Internet. It sounded creepy. I've always regarded the Internet as a meeting place for those who under normal circumstances cannot meet anybody. Now, that can be due to several reasons: it could be that they're so insecure they never have the guts to ask anyone out, or they might have such a bad personality that their occasional dates excuse themselves to go to the bathroom and never return to the table, or perhaps they're just plain busy and don't find the time to look for that special someone (that's what we all like to think).

But when you're desperate like me, you willingly compromise all your principles and do things that you never imagined you could possibly do. Actually, this might work out good for me since I can lie in the comfort of my house and tell women exactly what they want to hear without any hesitation. It truly makes lying easy when you don't have to look the other person in the eyes. Now, I understand that people tend to downplay their physical limitations on the Internet, but you never know.

I was hoping that a nourishing and virtuous woman was waiting to be blessed by my presence on the Internet. If that woman happened to be a keyboard-banger, so be it.

I launched my browser one night, typed in the address, and got online. There were many categories to choose from; I picked the obvious one, "Find Your Soul Mate." I picked "Middle Eastern lover" as my login name and got sucked immediately into the chat room. Cyberladies, watch out! Here comes the Middle Eastern lover. There was only one other person in the chat room. Her name was "Lady Bug." It must be her lucky day, I thought.

Lady Bug==

Hey handsome. What's your name???

Middle Eastern lover==

Hi there. I'm the Middle Eastern lover. How are you doing, sweetheart?

Lady Bug==

Oh my ... the Middle Eastern lover! I'm sweating already. Are U a bad boy? Are U going to spank me?

Middle Eastern lover==

Spank you??? I don't like to spank my soul mate. I'm a gentleman with principles. I never raise my hand ... why do you want me to spank you anyway?

Lady Bug==

I like to be spanked when I'm nutty. I get out of line sometimes and need to be punished by big burly Middle Eastern men.

Middle Eastern lover===

Well, if you insist. I personally think violence is not the answer. A relationship grows when both parties know their place, their role and functionality.

Lady Bug==

Oh yes. I like a man who's functional. I like a man who would tie me up and whip me every night. I
want a man who would dominate me and put me in place when I'm bad. I want a man who likes to play Fireman or Doctor.

Middle Eastern lover==

I always wanted to be a Doctor!!

Lady Bug==

Oh my... do you have a big thermometer???

Middle Eastern lover==

I have a digital thermometer!

Lady Bug==

Oh yeah, you're getting me hot.

Middle Eastern Lover==

So, what's your favorite sport?

Lady Bug==

Sword fighting.

Middle Eastern Lover==

Your favorite food?

Lady Bug==

Polish sausage.

Middle Eastern Lover==
Your favorite book?

Lady Bug==
Moby Dick.

Middle Eastern Lover==
Moby Dick by Herman Melville?

Lady Bug==
No. Moby Dick by Moby.

Middle Eastern Lover==
You sure sound exciting. I'm impressed.

Lady Bug==
Oh, you've no idea how exciting I can be. You too sure sound like my kinda guy. I want you to rough me up and smack me hard—YOU BIG BOY. I want you to hang me upside down and piss on me.

Middle Eastern Lover==
What? Piss on you?!!!

Lady Bug==
Oh yeah? Now, you tell me what you desire baby,
you can tell me anything.

Middle Eastern lover==
I want a woman I can take home to my mom. A woman who would take care of my kids, cook, clean. I want a virgin. A woman who is modern, yet traditional.

Lady Bug==

A woman!?....what the hell do you mean A WOMAN!?

Middle Eastern lover==

A woman, you know? A lovely, soft, delicious woman.

Lady Bug==

This is a GAY chat room... U f*@##*% MORON!

3. How I Met My Ex-wife

I MET MY EX-WIFE IN COLLEGE. She was it. She was cool, pretty, charming, and popular—pretty much everything that I wasn't. She was young and naïve which was a good thing since young girls lack intuition and can't detect character flaws in men. She was also fun to be around.

Being the vain Middle Eastern man that I am, I spent most of my time at college in the gym instead of the classroom. I looked good in my clothes and looked even better naked.

A group of young, well-to-do Middle Eastern college kids were sitting at a table in Starbucks near the campus. Girls in little cute bellbottoms, guys with George Clooney haircuts and goatees, BMWs parked outside, tall espresso supremos in hand, cell phones lined up on the table. It was all so sexy.

A political discussion on the Middle East crisis was flaring out of control. Passion and anger filled the room. The air was heavy. People were going at it. Everybody was an expert.

I was sitting with them not because I knew anything about politics or gave a shit about Israel or Palestine. I was there because I had my eyes on this cute little girl (my future wife) with the biggest you-know-whats. She was my dream girl. A petite Iranian babe, groomed in all the right places—big brown eyes and a smile that lights up the bedroom (did I say bedroom? I meant the room).

She was passionate about Israel, and her then so-called boyfriend was pro-Palestine. They were arguing like a married couple. I was enjoying the whole thing. This was good stuff. I thought, "Boy, if I could just get my hands on her, politics would be the last thing on her mind."

I find politics sickening. I especially don't care much about the current Middle East crisis. What crisis? Just because you happened to be from that part of the world, the issue doesn't automatically become important to you. Besides, this has been going on for years. How did it become a crisis all of a sudden? The reason I don't care is because I'm not there. Hey, shoot me, at least I'm honest. My philosophy is "mind over matter"; if you don't mind, it doesn't matter. In addition, I had more pressing issues on my mind at the moment, like how to get this little Iranian honey into my apartment.

I got a feeling that her so-called boyfriend was suspicious of my intentions toward his woman. He was a jerk. One of those Iranian dudes who knew everything. A preppy jackass with an attitude. He was rich and handsome, and that made me hate him even more. The boyfriend knew about my little nutty (Fantasy Island) dreams involving his girlfriend. He was giving me the look. You know? THE LOOK. Well, I didn't care. He spent his time in the classroom. I spent my time at the gym. I was much bigger than he was. I could snap his little preppy neck with a twist of my wrist.

The boyfriend was staring at me; I was staring at his girlfriend and drooling. He pointed at me and said, "So, what do you think about this mess?"

"Who, me?" I replied.

"Yes, you."

"What mess?" I said.

"You know, the Middle East crisis. You must have an opinion on the subject."

Bastard got me. I could kill him. I looked at my future wife. She was looking at me with those incredibly adorable eyes. Damn, I'm horny, I thought to myself.

"Well, I think the Israelis should kick Palestinian ass," I replied, while looking at the cute girl.

She smiled at me. Score. I'm in. The whole room went quiet.

"And you call that justice?" the boyfriend said.

"I guess."

"You guess?"

He wouldn't let go. He wanted a piece of me. He was trying to get me to make an ass of myself (to accomplish that, all you have to do is to give me alcohol and step back).

"Hey, man, I ain't an expert, but in order for this conflict to end, somebody has to win. So I pick Israel. They are stronger. The strong survive. It's nature's way of solving conflicts."

The girl smiled again. I flexed my biceps. Life was good.

"What kind of an idiotic theory is that?" the boyfriend asked.

Under normal circumstances his body would have been floating in his coffee mug by then. However, I didn't want to turn off my future wife by displaying my bad temper—yet.

"Hey, man, whatever floats your boat. I'm just expressing my opinion."

"You're a Zionist."

I didn't even know what that meant, but it sounded cool.

"Hell, whatever you say."

The future wife was smiling and giving me facial expressions that said, "I taste like ice-cream, big boy. Come and have some."

I felt my muscles ripping through my shirt. I wanted some of that.

"Listen, people like you make the world a difficult place to live for the rest of us intelligent beings," the boyfriend shouted.

Okay, that did it. I grabbed him by the neck and picked him off the chair like a rag doll. He started to turn blue.

"Listen, man, I don't care about your politics. I don't care about your values or anything. I just wanna shag your girlfriend. That's all."

I couldn't believe I'd said that. Everyone in the whole coffee shop was staring at me. You could have heard a pin drop. I put the guy back down on his chair. He gasped for air. My future wife looked up at me with the biggest smile and said, "I'm so flattered. Nothing like this has ever happened to me before."

Oh yeah. Who's your daddy?

"You wanna get out of here? Say we go to my apartment and discuss politics?" I asked.

"I would love to."

That's how we met, but dating her was big pain in the ass. Let me explain: I'm not the smartest guy out there, and when God was teaching her creatures common sense, I was at the gym.

They say, "The path to success comes from being either book-smart or street-smart." My problem is that I don't read much, and I almost never wander the streets. But the key word is "smart," which is something that I am not very familiar with. However, the weakest weapon in my limited arsenal must be my social skills. My lack of social skills didn't become apparent to me until I started dating my wife, who happened to be Iranian.

Dating an American woman does not require many social skills or trickery. First of all, you don't have to deal with her dad, mom, brothers, sisters, cousins, aunts, uncles, grandparents, nieces, nephews, family friends, neighbors, butcher, milkman, etc. Dating an American woman is like a game of tennis. It's one on one. Chances are pretty good that her parents live in some faraway state and she has limited contact, if any, with her immediate family. That makes life so much easier.

However, dating an Iranian woman is like a game of soccer. You constantly bump into other players. It's a full-contact sport. Unexpected slide tackles, violent kicks, tripping, pushing and shoving are all common.

It was easy for me to get away with just about anything with American women so long as I used being a foreigner as an excuse. "Sorry, babe, I didn't know remembering birthdays is an American tradition. Thank you for educating me on this." Or, "Oh, really? So you buy flowers on Valentine's Day?"

I also made up cultural lies like, "Honey, going out to nightclubs with the boys till three a.m. and coming home shit-faced is an old Iranian tradition that goes back three thousand years. You know I'm a fool for tradition." Or, "We Iranians get in touch with our inner self by taking road trips to Las Vegas."

But, my future wife didn't let me get away with anything. She just didn't buy any of my lies.

For a person like me who always looks for shortcuts in life, dating my future wife was a great chore. But at the time she was important to me. She was beautiful and kind, and her dad was loaded. I'm talking money growing on trees in the back yard.

So I knew that I had to modify my behavior for the time being and act as normal as I possibly could to get her to marry me. But there was so much that I didn't know. I had so many questions. Therefore, I sought help from my cousin, Reza, aka *El Cheapo*, who claimed to be an authority on dating Iranian women.

I told Reza I needed help developing strategy to avoid roadblocks thrown at me mostly by her family. I required a solid plan to keep my then future wife, now ex-wife, interested, fascinated, even infatuated. I told Reza that I would do anything, and I'd go to any lengths to get this chick to fall in love with me.

Reza asked me to meet him at a coffee shop. He ordered a large java and sat down in front of me. He was looking at me like my fifth-grade math teacher. I was waiting for him to throw something at me.

"Remember, an Iranian woman feels loved and secure when the family respects her boyfriend," Reza said. "Demand respect by projecting a false and pretentious self-image. Make her family think you are destined for greatness. Avoid conversations that require actual knowledge of the subject. Always show up late for events or gatherings. Always carry a key chain with a BMW or Porsche logo on it; leave the key chain somewhere visible to everyone."

I cut him off. "Whoa, slow down, man. What does a key chain have to do with anything?"

"You date American girls," Reza barked. "You don't understand how Iranian girls operate. It's all about family with these girls. You get accepted by the family, you are automatically accepted by her."

El Cheapo looked serious now. He looked as if he was explaining rocket science to a five-year-old.

"I'm going to share with you years of experience in dating Iranian women. Just listen and shut up." He sipped his coffee and continued, "Never say to an Iranian woman, 'My mom's shish kabob is better than your mom's.' Always compliment her mom's cooking even if you spent the whole night hugging the toilet bowl after one of her dinner parties. When discussing weight-loss programs with her mom, never say 'You want to lose weight? How about staying off that basmati rice for the next 20 years?' Always tell her mom how beautiful she looks. When it comes to gossiping, NEVER out-perform her mom. Always look interested in what her mom says even if she repeats herself a hundred times. Tell her mom that your aspiration in life is to help orphaned children."

"What are you talking about?" I asked.

"Shut up. I know what I'm talking about," Reza said. "Charm her dad by using meaningless words while discussing politics. Tell him that all our problems are a direct result of foreign interventions in Iran's internal affairs during the last five hundred years. Blame everything on the British or the Americans and reassure him that his generation had nothing to do with the problems that the Middle East faces today. Boost her dad's ego by mentioning—several times—how impressive his Mercedes Benz looks and what a great house he owns. Never greet her dad by saying 'WAZZZZUUUPPP' or 'YO, how's it hangin'?' Tell her dad you are seriously considering medical school."

"Medical school?" I asked.

"Well, you and I know damn well that your GPA isn't good enough to even get you to a culinary school, but they don't have to know that. Tell her dad you are negotiating intensely for that high-level management position and your job at the gas station is only a hobby."

"Are you kidding me? Nobody buys this crap," I said.

"Listen to me, I'm giving you the gold," Reza said. He was getting serious now. He looked like someone possessed by some magical power.

He sipped his coffee eagerly and rambled on. "Never tell her brother, 'Dude, what're you thinking? Everybody knows you meet psychos on the Internet.'"

"Didn't you meet your girlfriend on the Internet?" I said.

"Do not interrupt me," Reza said. "Speak to her brother as an equal, even though you think he's the biggest dork on the face of the planet. Try not to laugh when he tells you he has a doctorate from some Caribbean university. Wipe the smile off your face before telling him that your interest in his sister is emotional, not sexual. When you're at a nightclub with him, don't jump out of your seat and say, 'Ouch, I'd like to get me some of that ass.' Tell him you have made a small fortune in the market by investing in blue chips."

"What's a blue chip?" I asked Reza.

"I'm not exactly sure, but it sounds impressive."

I was confused. This was way too much for me to remember, and some of it sounded fishy. I stood up and thanked him for his time.

"Wait, I haven't covered the rest of the family yet."

"I'm outta here."

In spite of my cousin Reza's IQ being only a couple of notches above the IQ of a tennis ball, I decided to apply his strategy. I had nothing to lose and so much to gain. Even though none of what he said made any sense, I took his advice and started lying and deceiving my future wife and her family. I kissed her family's ass till my lips turned red and swollen. I gave it a hundred and ten percent and went out of my way to make her family feel special. I treated her like a queen. I gave and gave, and to my surprise, it finally worked. My wife gave in to my charm, and despite her family's intense opposition, she married me. After that it was all downhill.

I never knew how difficult married life could be. Like a typical Middle Eastern man, the idea of being married was attractive to me, but the actual state of being married is a whole different story. Nothing can really prepare you for what comes next. But one thing is clear to me now: marriage is no place for a lazy guy. It's hard work. My marriage was nothing short of an ongoing pursuit of perfection—especially when it came to satisfying my wife. Like I said, marriage is no place for lazy guys like me.

One big obstacle in our marriage was my constant inability to find The Spot. My wife was a maniac in bed, and I was exhausted all the time, trying to do the right thing. There were several times when I truly thought that I was having cardiac arrest while trying to make my wife happy.

I falsely believed that my wife's constant appetite for animal engagements in bed would die fast after the first year of marriage. That's what I'd heard from all my married friends. But that was not the case.

It was ironic: most of my married friends were complaining about total lack of intimacy and animal sex with their wives, and I was on the verge of full physical breakdown from too much intimacy.

So I went on doing what I could to make the wife happy. But it just did not work. I could not find the G-spot. That's right, folks. For the life of me, I could not find the damn thing. Forget about it. I don't even think it exists. I'm convinced that women have made it up to watch men act like bunch of idiots.

It's not like my life wasn't complicated enough or I had no problems of my own to deal with, now I had to worry about finding a small organ buried under lumps of epidermis.

What's going on here? Is this another one of nature's cruel jokes on me? We have invented devices that help us find our way around just about anything. We have invented topographic maps, compasses, radar, smart bombs, and GPS systems which can pinpoint locations and lead us to our destinations with deadly accuracy.

So how come no one has invented a G-spot positioning system? A device that could help me locate the offending object without making an ass out of myself in front of my wife. I'm talking some kind of a 007 gadget that would lead me straight to the target: Beep beep beep beep beep beep beep beeeep. BINGO!

Don't get me wrong. I did put in my share of enthusiasm in this whole "intimate relationship" thing; but give me a break. It was ridiculous.

As far as the wife was concerned, I was a complete failure in life and in bed.

Our families' relationship was also another factor that contributed to the failure of our marriage. My parents hated the queen bitch's parents, and there were always frictions during family gatherings. Family plays an important role in the survival of a Middle Eastern-American marriage. If families get along, things can get a little easier, but if families don't see eye-to-eye on issues, then you might as well kiss your marriage goodbye.

In our case, family closeness had nothing to do with family or closeness. It was not as much about caring or loving as it was about an uncontrollable desire to know about each other's business. It was a surveillance tactic to keep an eye on the other members of the clan. It was a great tool to find out who's doing what. It was important for my wife's family to know who was doing better than them and why. It also gave my family momentous satisfaction and comfort knowing that the in-laws were as screwed up as they were. It made them feel better about themselves.

Growing up in an Iranian family, in early adolescence we had to constantly measure up. There was intense competition between us and the other kids in the extended family. A cutthroat competition, fueled by our parents.

We were forced to strive for academic greatness. Nothing wrong with that except our parents didn't care much about us learning as long as we were getting good grades.

They measured success based on how well their kids did at school in comparison to the nieces and nephews.

It's what I call educational show-off. It's not really important if our children are a bunch of unimaginative, social retards as long as they are academically out-performing their cousins. And if they are not, all hell will break lose. "Olaagh (jackass). Look at your cousins. They're getting all A's at school. They're the top students in their class, and you are flunking every subject. Idiot, you're not my son, I'm sure the milkman stopped by."

Our parents continued to mess up our heads under the umbrella of family closeness. We observed and learned our parents' pretentious demeanors and applied them in our own lives. When the time came for us to choose our mates and start our own families, our parents set arrogant standards for us to follow.

Guys in the family had to bring in brides blessed with incomparable beauty, wealth and education. And of course, all the girls in the family had to marry rich guys. We all want millionaires attached to the family tree. No one wants to take a poor schmuck to a family party and introduce him as the son-in-law. Imagine all the laughs and rumors.

Once we started our own family, we were officially initiated into the delicate and strategic alliance whose sole purpose was obtaining information—sneaky information about other members of the family. Information about who's pregnant, who's dating, who's screwing, whose marriage's falling apart, whose kids are on crack cocaine, who's happy, who's miserable, who's faithful, who's cheating, who's sick.

A good example would be the time that the father-in-law threw a big party for his son's college graduation. My wife's family would go to any length to show off their wealth, and they made a point of constantly reminding my family of my failures in life. It didn't bother me, but it pissed off my parents tremendously. I figured my ultimate revenge was marrying their daughter.

During the graduation party, my dad had a little too much to drink and started telling stories about his younger years when he was a champion wrestler.

"All you young guys are a bunch of wusses. When I was your age, I was a national legend in Iran. People asked for my autograph everywhere I went."

"How come I never heard of you?" my father-in-law shouted from across the room.

"Because you are deaf," my dad responded, slamming his drink on the table.

My dad wrestled his siblings in the backyard of his parents' house when he was a youngster in Iran, but he certainly wasn't close to being a national legend. He was big for his age, and he was known for bullying smaller kids in the neighborhood. In his late teens, my dad tried out for a wrestling team, but he was so bad that the coach suggested he look into playing a sport with less contact, such as Ping-Pong.

"My wrestling matches against some of the greatest Turkish and Russian wrestlers were televised live all over the nation," my father said.

Now that was a total lie.

"How come I never saw you on television?" my father-in-law asked.

"Because you are blind."

"I think you are full of shit," my father-in-law said.

My father took a long sip of his drink and said to my father-in-law in a threatening tone, "Full of shit? I bet I still can kick your ass. Of course, wrestling is out of the question since I'll probably break every bone in your body. How about arm wrestling?"

This was a calculated move by my dad to put my father-in-law on the spot.

My father-in-law, who was a legend in his own mind, could not allow this one to slide by. He knew that my father was trying to make a fool out of him in front of his guests, and if he didn't accept the challenge, he would be regarded as a coward and lose face among his admirers. Even though he was on several hundred medications and had one foot practically in the grave, he accepted the challenge. This was not good.

Now, picture a seventy-eight-year-old man arm wrestling an eighty-two-year-old man. It was ugly.

My father sat down at one end of a small table, my father-in-law sat at the other end with his oxygen tank by his side. They looked deep into each other's eyes, locked hands, and went at it. The arm-wrestling match was on.

My father was being cheered on by his side of the family and my father-in-law was being cheered on by his side. People started betting on the event. A bookie collected money and began putting names down in his notebook. I placed a fifty on my dad.

My wife, the "Bitcha Grande," was looking at me from across the room with the most hateful look on her face. I knew she blamed the whole thing on me, and I was most likely sleeping on the couch that night. No matter what the outcome, I was the loser in this match. I had to stop this madness. I had to quickly think of something.

My dad and my father-in-law were both about to pass out, but neither one would let go. They were two proud Middle Eastern men who knew very well that defeat in this contest meant complete social disrespect for many years to come. This was a matter of pride, and nobody questions a Middle Eastern man's manhood.

I looked around the room. I needed to find something to help me stop the clash of the egomaniac geriatrics. I found my nerdy brother-in-law standing in the back, biting nervously on his fingernails.

I slowly walked behind him, covered his mouth with my hand, dragged him out in the backyard, and pushed him into the swimming pool. My flimsy brother-in-law, who never learned how to swim, started to scream like a little girl. The poor guy was drowning. It seemed pretty entertaining at the time.

Distracted by my brother-in-law's wild cry for help, everybody ran out into the back yard. My dad and father-in-law took immediate advantage of the situation and disengaged. A draw was the best thing that could have happened to them in this situation.

My mother-in-law dove into the pool, trying to save her beloved boy. The problem was that she didn't know how to swim either. They were both drowning now. I wish I had had a camcorder.

There were a number of guests who had expensive suits on and didn't show any willingness to jump into the pool and ruin their high-priced attire. I, too, had my Pierre Cardin shirt on, and there was no way in hell I was going to damage it to save my in-laws' lives.

I found a floaty by the pool. I throw it in and yelled, "Hold on to this and kick to the edge."

My mother-in-law and her son grabbed the floaty and kicked with their legs until they reached the shallow part of the pool.

My brother-in-law got out of the pool and began chasing me around the house. He kept yelling, "He did it. He tried to kill me. He did it."

That event did not sit well with my wife's family. My wife wasn't very impressed by the stunt either, and she did not talk to me for six months. This is what I get for being a nice guy, trying to keep the family together. As I said, no matter who started the conflict or who finished it, I was the real loser.

4. My Wife's Best Friend

THERE ARE CERTAIN INDIVIDUALS who sometimes leave irreparable marks on your relationships. These individuals mysteriously appear and basically destroy everything that is good in your life. Not that anything was going right in my relationship with the wife, but now I had to deal with this pain-in-the-ass Susan chick.

Susan was my wife's best friend and came into our lives out of nowhere. Susan and my wife were together twenty-four hours a day. They went shopping together, they spent hours in coffee shops drinking latté and socializing together, they worked out together and they even shared clothing and accessories. I found the whole affair unusual.

Susan was a very tall, skinny Iranian woman with a ghostly face and a nasty temper. She was the type that looked at men as if she wanted to chew them up and spit them out. Her facial expression was one of constant anger. Susan handled herself with amazing confidence and she didn't take crap from men. Like many healthy Iranian men out there, I hate women like that. They scare me. The majority of us men prefer women who act needy. It makes us feel wanted. I'm just telling you the truth.

My suspicions grew as I came across certain things that did not make any sense. For example, I would walk into the house and find Susan and my wife in the bedroom with the door locked. They would later come out and claim that they were trying on new clothes. Or there were times when I would walk into the living room and the two of them would stop talking and stare at me with obvious revulsion.

My wife met Susan at the gym and somewhere between Pilates and yoga class they became best friends. My wife said that they hit it off right away and became soul mates. She claimed that when she first laid eyes on Susan, she felt that they had met in a previous life. Oh, give me a break.

Ever since Susan, "the Homebreaker," walked into our lives, my relationship with the wife became shoddier by the minute. My wife was acting strangely around me and the passion was gone altogether. I felt that Susan was feeding my wife all kinds of negative thoughts, and she encouraged my wife to turn against me. The wife and I would have intense fights right after Susan had stepped out of our house. That did not sit well with me, and I was ready to kick some serious ass. I mean, where did this woman come from and what does she want from me?

So, I consulted the only man I could trust with this delicate matter: my father. The man had lived a long time, and I figured he must have picked up some experience along the way.

My father is not exactly the most reliable source for advice but he was all I had. So I explained the situation to him. He stared at me and shook his head, "I knew she was up to no good. I told you before you married her."

"It's a little too late for that, Dad. What should I do? I mean this beast of a woman is really messing things up for me. I feel like she is filling my wife's head with all kinds of garbage."

"Are you blind?" my old man said. "Don't you see what's going on?"

"What?"

"They are plotting against you. They are obviously lovers, and they're plotting to kill you."

"Lovers? Like lesbians?" I replied.

"Sure."

"Really? Like women kissing and stuff?"

"Sure," my father said.

"Well, the lesbian part, I don't mind," I said. "But getting killed is definitely a problem."

"It's very obvious. They're plotting to kill you, dump your body in the river, claim the insurance money and move out of the country."

"What insurance money?" I said.

"Don't you have life insurance?" My father asked.

"No."

"Are you sure? Are you really sure?"

"I don't know," I said.

"You know she can get a life insurance policy on you without you even knowing it."

"She can?"

"Sure. Lots of wives do that before killing their husbands," my father said. "Your mother wanted to try that. She kept telling me to go get a life insurance policy."

"Did you get one?"

"Are you crazy? Life insurance is the number one cause of men's deaths."

"So, you're saying that my wife is having an affair with another woman and she is going to kill me?"

"Exactly," my father said. "I have seen it many times before. I bet her father has put her up to this, that old bastard."

"Dad, that's absurd," I said.

"Is it? What do you think they're doing in the bedroom with the door locked, huh? What do you think they talk about behind your back, huh? Boy, you're history."

"What do I do?"

"Son, you have come to the right man. I'm a bit of an expert on this matter."

"You are? How?"

"I had a neighbor back in Iran who had the same problem. His wife got her groove on with the next-door neighbor guy and together they plotted to kill the poor husband."

"Are you making this up?" I asked.

"No, I'm serious. It was in the papers."

"So what happened?"

"What happened? Two months later, they found the husband's head in the next town. He was in a real bad shape," my father said.

"Real bad shape? What do you mean 'real bad shape'? The guy's head was cut off! You are not making this up? Are you?"

"Of course not. Would I lie to you?"

"Yes."

"Oh, that's cold," My father said, walking away.

"Okay, sorry, Dad. I'm just a bit confused."

"I don't blame you. I would've been confused, too, if I just found out that my wife is a killer lesbian."

"So, what do you suggest I should do?" I asked.

"It's her damn father. I know these things. He is behind the whole thing."

"Come on, man. Leave the father-in-law out of this. I know you have your differences, but I need you to focus on my problems, not yours," I said.

"Boy, I can't believe you're my son. You're too stupid to see what's in front of your nose. Her old man is setting you up."

"Dad, stop it."

"Okay, fine. Here is what you do. The best defense is a strong offense. You shall utilize the elements of surprise. She is not expecting any counterattacks and that's exactly what you will do," my father said.

"Counterattack? I like it. How?"

"Simple. You beat her at her own game."

"How is that?"

"Go to a gay club and pick up one of them good looking boys. A big fruity one. Then you hang out with the guy all the time. Make sure she sees you. Lock yourself in the room with the dude and do things that them gay boys do like a pillow fight, or slap each other on the ass. That works every time."

"What?"

"Let me finish," my father said. "This behavior will confuse her. It will throw her off. If she asks you what the hell is going on, tell her the guy is just a buddy."

"Are you out of your mind?" I said. "Do you even know what you're talking about?"

"Yes, I do," my father said.

"You're telling me to go pick up a gay man and do role-plays in front of my wife?"

"Yes. That way she'll think that you're plotting to kill her. That would completely change the dynamics of the game."

I realized at that moment that my father was way overdue for a comprehensive mental health checkup.

"Dad, thank you for the advice. I'll keep that in mind," I said, walking away.

"Hey, boy, if you can't find a good-looking gay man, don't worry too much about it. I think your mother's nephew is gay. I'll talk to him. I'm sure he'll be more than happy to help."

"That's okay, Dad. Please don't do a thing."

I was extremely confused. The idea of my wife plotting with another woman to kill me was absolutely ridiculous, but my father had managed to successfully plant the seed of suspicion in my mind and I couldn't shake it off. I needed to find out exactly what was going on with Susan and my wife. Why take a chance?

I figured the best way to tackle this problem was to think and act like a politician. How do you make people look bad in front of others? You question their credibility. So, I figured the only way I could get Susan out of our lives was to sabotage her relationship with my wife by assassinating her character.

To achieve this, I needed careful planning and vigilant implementation. So I started to monitor Susan's activities around our house. Every time Susan showed up at our house, I quietly removed an item of clothing from my wife's closet—nothing big, just small items. It didn't take long before my wife noticed certain items of her clothing were missing.

"Have you seen my blue shirt?" my wife asked.

"Your blue shirt? No, haven't seen it."

"It was hanging in the closet yesterday."

"Yeah, I think I saw it in there. I'm sure you'll find it," I said.

"This is really strange. My brown skirt is also missing."

"Well, I'll let you know if I see them."

Things started to get out of hand. Her underwear, socks and shoes were also missing now. The wife was beginning to freak out. The plan was working perfectly.

I also contacted my friend, Jose, who played on my soccer team and worked for the U.S. Immigration Service to do a background check on Susan. I had this strange feeling that she might have been an illegal immigrant. My suspicion was confirmed. Jose, after some research, told me that she came to the U.S. on a student visa twelve years ago, and she has been illegally staying here for the past eight years. I told Jose that I had some good news.

Now it was time to take it to the next level. One day, while Susan and my wife were in our bedroom doing whatever they normally did in there, I shoved one of my wife's skirts in Susan's purse. I intentionally left a small portion of the skirt out so it could be easily spotted. I was beginning to scare myself. I was way too good at this.

My wife and Susan finally came out of the bedroom. My wife saw the purse and recognized her skirt. She froze.

"Is that my skirt in your purse?" my wife asked Susan.

"Sorry?" Susan replied.

"That's my skirt. What is it doing in your purse?"

Susan turned red. She was totally confused, "Oh, gosh, I'm not sure how that got in my purse. I'm stumped."

"Have you been taking my stuff?"

"Your stuff?" Susan said. "I'm not sure what you're talking about."

"My stuff has been missing in the last few weeks. You have been stealing my stuff."

"Excuse me?" Susan said.

"You have been stealing my clothes and shoes. It all makes sense now. Every time you come here, something goes missing," my wife said.

"Are you crazy? Why would I steal your ugly stuff? I wouldn't wear that skirt if you paid me."

"Bullshit. You have taken advantage of my kindness and hospitality. All the things that I have done for you, and this is how you pay me back?"

"I would never do that."

"Oh, yeah, then how do you explain this? I want you out of my house," my wife said.

"Are you accusing me of stealing your clothes?"

"Yes, I am," my wife said.

"Fine. Here is your hideous skirt. I'm out of here."

Score! As Susan stepped out of the house, she was intercepted and taken down by INS agents in the front yard of our house. Jose and his boys arrested Susan for staying illegally in the U.S. and they violently handcuffed her. The witch was gone. Susan's ghostly face looked even whiter and sicker than before.

My wife watched Susan as she was shoved into the INS car and taken away. This was a great moment. I had my revenge. Damn, I'm good!

"Do you believe this woman? Staying here illegally and stealing from us," I told my wife.

"I'm puzzled," my wife said. "I thought she was a totally different person."

"I hear you. I mean, you can't trust people nowadays."

"I know. After all the things I did for her."

"What exactly did you do for her?" I asked.

"Well, you are not supposed to know," my wife said.

"It's okay. I know you guys were lovers," I said.

"Excuse me?"

"I know everything and I forgive you."

"Forgive me?" my wife said. "Forgive me for what?"

"For having an affair with her and plotting to kill me."

"What?"

"It was very obvious. But we don't have to talk about it anymore. That chapter can be closed," I said.

"Wait a minute. What the hell are you talking about?"

"Listen, I know what you guys did in the bedroom with the door locked. You think I'm stupid. You guys were doing it in there."

"Doing what?" my wife wanted to know.

"Doing the thing, you know, the nasty," I said.

"You stupid idiot! Susan has cancer. That's why she looks so thin and pale. She came over to our house to get her injections. We would go in the bedroom and I would give her three injections for her cancer treatments."

"Cancer?"

"Yes, cancer."

"What about those quiet conversations in the living room, and what about going mute as soon as I walked in?" I asked.

"She is a very private person, and she didn't want people to know about her condition," my wife said. "So every time you walked in on our conversation about her illness, we would stop. I just don't understand why she would steal my clothes."

"Oh, God."

"What?"

"Oh, man."

"What did you do?" my wife said.

"I swear I didn't know. I thought you guys were planning to kill me. Oh, man."

"Why would you think that?"

"My dad told me. He said I was history. I set her up," I said.

"Set her up? What do you mean?"

"She didn't steal anything. I stole all your clothes. I planted your skirt in her purse. I called the INS on her. Man, I feel like a jackass."

"How could you do that?"

"I don't know. I was scared."

"You are a jackass," my wife said, storming out of the room.

"I'm sorry. I didn't know."

How could I be so blind? I ruined the woman's life. She will probably be deported back to Iran. What kind of an animal would do this to another human being? And she has cancer. What did I do?

I became conscious of the fact that paranoia had taken over my life and affected my judgments. It took me a few days to get over it, but my wife was confounded by my actions. She tried to get Susan a lawyer and sponsor her to stay in the country, but her efforts were fruitless and Susan got deported. I felt really bad about that episode, and if I could do it all over again, I would skip the INS part.

5. The Day I Killed My Father-in-law

MY MARRIAGE WAS FALLING APART after a few years. It was very apparent to both me and the wife that things were not working out between us. With two additions to our family, things got even worse.My wife's family just plain hated me. The feeling was mutual. But the day I killed my father-in-law was pretty much the nail in the coffin. My marriage was over after that.

Honoring the grand Iranian tradition of butt kissing, I visited my father-in-law to pay my respects on his birthday. My father-in-law was a traditional man, and he, like most traditional Iranian men, had an ego grander than the Grand Canyon. I had to constantly feed his ego by praising his very existence while making him feel important and needed.

This, of course, put my wife in a good mood, which was important to our marital relationship at the time since her bitch meter was mostly running on high RPM. Making sure that my wife was in a good mood was the single most important task in our household. It also brought calm and quiet to our life, which was something that came around once every century.

My father-in-law was a very rich man who had many children and grandchildren. This situation had prompted stiff competition among all the family members to stay on good terms with the old man for a small matter of a few million dollars in inheritance money which could land in someone's lap any day now. This matter had made brown nosing and ass kissing the sport of choice, and since we Iranians have mastered this ancient art, the competition was fierce, cruel, and shameless.

I, on the other hand, did not share the enthusiasm displayed by the rest of the family for my father-in-law's money, and I found the man arrogant, selfish, and annoying. He had made his great fortune by cunningly swindling the poor and needy out of their money, lending them cash in times of trouble and charging high interest in return.

The feeling was mutual since my father-in-law hated my guts and couldn't stand seeing me with his daughter. He believed that his girl deserved someone much better. And she should have married a dentist or a doctor just like the rest of his daughters did. He thought that I was completely clueless when it came to money.

Perhaps he was correct. When it comes to money management or financial know-how, I'm as knowledgeable as a baboon. I'll be the first to admit that I'm ignorant about anything that remotely resembles, smells, or feels like money. The way I see it, a dollar earned today is a dollar already spent last week. My savings consist of quarters and pennies that have fallen out of my pockets between the sofa cushions.

It doesn't matter how much money I make, how many raises I get, or how many times I switch jobs; I'm always fifty bucks short at the end of the month. I'm also illiterate about financial planning like 401K, money market accounts, retirement plans, and the like. Forget about it. Retirement is for old people. I'm young, and I'm on a mission to spend as much money as I possibly can for the purpose of self-gratification. My wife wanted me to come up with a serious action plan for my retirement. I thought it was a good idea, so I learned golf.

On the other hand, all my in-laws were rich and successful. They had managed to accumulate, among other things, healthy portfolios of stocks, bonds, and real estate. So as you can see, I was the one who needed to kiss my father-in-law's rear end 24/7. And that's exactly the point my wife made all the time. As much as I hate to admit it, she had a good point. I needed to step on my pride, take a deep breath, stick my nose deep in the old man's bottom and secure our future. It was time for action.

I approached the old man at his birthday party and asked him for a moment of his time. He gave me one of his hateful looks and reluctantly accepted. He ordered me to follow him to his private room. He sat down in his favorite chair and said, "What the hell do you want?"

"Listen, old man, let me get right to the point. You and I both know that you are loaded. Frankly, you don't look good. Looking at you, I don't find you all that healthy. It's just a matter of time before you kick the bucket and meet your maker. I, personally, am amazed to see you alive with all that smoking and that unhealthy diet of yours. But that's beside the point. I need to know how much inheritance money your daughter and I will get after you meet the big guy upstairs. I'm here to negotiate. I know it's kind of unorthodox, but I think, as two mature individuals, we should be able to work out a deal and come up with a figure that is mutually acceptable."

I noticed my father-in-law turning red. He started breathing heavily and was looking around to find something substantial to throw at me. He tried to stand up, but he was overwhelmed with anger and unable to move. He eventually got his composure back and whispered, "You son of a bitch. I will kill you before you get a penny of my money. I will hire a hit man to put you out of your misery. I will—"

I cut him off and said, "Yeah, I'm really scared. Listen, things have been kind of bad for me lately. Life is extremely expensive. Flying to Las Vegas every weekend with the guys, gambling, chasing women, nudie bars, drinking, partying, traveling, expensive cars. It all takes a good deal of money. To make things easy, I will throw a number at you—let's say, oh, a million dollars, and we can base our negotiations on that. What do you say?"

My father-in-law looked terrifying. He started breathing hard again. He made strange noises and rocked from side to side. He grabbed his chest, coughed a few times, and fell back on his chair with his eyes rolled back. I walked closer to assess the situation. Holy cow! I'd killed the man! He was gone.

I ran out of the room screaming, "Call nine-one-one, He's gone, call nine-one-one."

Everybody at the party rushed into the room screaming with horror. They looked at the old man's body with disbelief.

"What happened here?" my brother-in-law asked.

"It was all so very dramatic," I said. "The old man came to me and kindly asked me to join him in his private room." I wiped the tears off my face and continued, "He sat on his favorite chair and told me how much he loved me and how much respect he had for me. He said that I was his favorite son-in-law. He said that I was bright and trustworthy. He was proud to have his daughter marry such a fine individual. He said that he wanted me to handle all his finances after he's gone. He wanted me to take over the family business and manage his will based on my own judgment and what I saw fit. He wanted me to carry the family legacy and make sure that you all get some money based on your needs. I cried and begged him to relieve me from such great responsibility, but he insisted. He wanted me to take the rest of his money and invest it for the good of the family. He just wanted me to be there for you all. I sure am gonna miss him. What a dear ... dear man."

My performance was Oscar-worthy, but the family did not buy my story, and all kinds of conspiracy theories started to develop. Some family members thought that I had strangled the old man to death. Other family members believed that I poisoned him, and some went so far as to accuse me of showing the old man pictures of his wife in bed with a younger man.

The father-in-law's funeral was another event that did not score me any points with the wife and her family.

I hate funerals. They remind me so much of my own mortality. The whole idea of being buried under tons of dirt is not appealing to me. Occasionally when I go to funerals, I picture myself trapped inside the coffin and it scares me to death. What if the county medical examiner screwed up and I'm still alive? Perhaps I'm in a coma and they think I'm dead.

It would suck to come out of a coma and find myself trapped in a box under 10 feet of mud. That's why, when I die, I would like to have a cell phone placed right next to my body—just in case. "Hello, dude, it's me. Listen, would you come down to the cemetery and get me out of here. I really need to go to the bathroom. No, I'm not dead. I was just in a coma."

I'm also scared of being cremated. The thought of being burned dead or alive is frightening to me. And I find the whole tradition of putting your remains inside an urn absolutely ridiculous. It's jut not very manly.

I'm sorry but certain religious beliefs just do not make any sense to me. I have a hard time believing in the concept of heaven and hell, and the idea of life after death is a bit unrealistic, if you ask me. I'm having a hard time buying a lot of stuff that has been sold to us in the name of religion. I know a number of people who don't even believe in organized religion and are damn good people, and I have come across religious folks who have the morality of a doorknob. So, I've come to the conclusion that practicing religion does not necessarily make you a good person.

I guess one thing about organized religion that turns me off the most is its followers' sense of self-righteousness and their tendency to believe that they have it all figured out.

I don't pray much and like many other people, I don't think about God too often, of course, unless I'm sick or I need something. I just don't buy the idea that a God who created this magnificent universe with everything in it would really need guys like me to worship her everyday unless, of course, she is extremely insecure and arrogant, which is highly unlikely.

My father-in-law's body was wrapped in a white sheet and placed in a wooden coffin. The coffin was placed on top of a metal holder, dangling over a big, dark hole. It was a somber moment. The crowd gathered around the coffin. I stayed in the back as instructed by my wife. My father-in-law was regarded in the community as a good Moslem. It did not make any sense since he practically raped the community by swindling desperate immigrants out of their money. But since he gave cash to the local mosque on a regular basis, he bought himself a place in heaven and the respect of the local religious people. It's amazing how money can buy you happiness in life, and a cozy place in heaven!

A middle-aged, high-profile mullah was sent from the local mosque to perform the service. The mullah walked towards the coffin and stood right next to it. He looked emotionless. It was business as usual.

"Jamal (my father-in-law's name) was a gift that was given to his family by God, and God took Jamal back from his family," the mullah said.

"Oh, brother," I whispered in the back.

The mullah turned around and looked at me. A few people coughed and looked away.

"Did you say something?" the mullah inquired.

"Come on, dude," I said. "You don't give somebody a gift and then turn around and take it back. That's considered rude. Why would God do something like that? That just doesn't make sense."

The mullah stared at me momentarily. He then turned his attention back to my dead father-in-law and continued, "Right now, Jamal is being met by two angels. He will be asked, 'who is your God?' and he will—"

"Give me a break," I interrupted the mullah. "You talk like you have been there. How do you know? Have you been dead before? Maybe he is being met by two midgets with bad teeth or a gang of nasty lesbians on motorcycles. Has anybody been dead and back to report all that? Did I miss something?"

The mullah looked clearly irritated. The family was looking at me with their eyes wide open. Other people started to distance themselves from me.

The mullah swallowed hard and continued, "When you are ready to meet your God, the last words that come to your mind before you die are 'God, I am at your mercy.'"

The mullah stopped and glanced at me as if he were waiting for a comment. The crowd looked on with anticipation. I was not about to disappoint the flock.

"I'm sorry, but if I'm having a heart attack and my chest is about to explode and I'm shitting in my pants, the last words on my mind would be more like 'Oh shit, call nine-one-one.'"

The mullah cleared his throat and continued, "Jamal's place belongs with the angels of God. His devotion to Allah will be rewarded by indulging the company of forty virgins in heaven—"

I couldn't let this one go. "Come on, dude, the man was over eighty years old, for God's sake. What could he possibly do with forty virgins? It's not like they have an endless supply of Viagra in heaven ... do they?"

That did it. My brother-in-law tried to attack me like a wild animal, but he was intercepted by other mourners before he could reach me. He was kicking and punching in the air, attempting to break loose from the crowd of people who were holding him down.

The mullah walked toward me, grabbed my arm, and whispered in my ear, "Listen, man, I do this part time, I'm a gym teacher at the YMCA and I drive a cab. Why are you sweating me like this? My wife's cheating on me, my son just told me he's gay, my daughter ran away with a motorcycle gang, and I have a hemorrhoid the size of a watermelon. Would you shut the hell up and let me finish?"

I was taken aback by the mullah's honesty. He was just another grifter, hustling to make Franklins like the rest of us.

My brother-in-law broke loose and started to chase me around the coffin. I could see murder in his eyes. I was running for my life. While pushing people out of the way, I tripped over a chair and bumped into the mullah. The mullah and I rocked backward and landed on top of my father-in-law's coffin. The support straps holding the coffin over the hole snapped and the coffin plunged into the hole with me and the mullah aboard. Since the mullah had never missed a meal in his life, his plump body cushioned my fall nicely.

Lying in the grave and looking up in the sky, I felt an unbelievable tranquility that I had never experienced before. It wasn't as bad inside the grave as I thought it would be. It was extremely peaceful and if it hadn't been because of the mullah's screaming due to a broken spine as the result of the impact, it would also have been very quiet in there. It became evident at that moment that the only place I'll ever find calm and serenity will be in the grave!

I asked the mullah if he was okay. He responded with words that I did not find particularly appropriate for a man of God.

My wife's family was staring down at me in disgust from the edge of the grave. I wished I could stay in there until everybody was gone, but I had to pee real bad.

6. She Is Gone

IT WAS A STORMY FRIDAY NIGHT. It was pouring outside. I came home from work and found the Dear John letter on the table. The letter was addressed to me:

Dear asshole,

I'm leaving you. I need some time to be alone. I need to reassess our marriage. I need my space. I need to breathe. I need to find myself.

I'm leaving you because, simply put, I hate you. I should've listened to my late father and married a dentist. You make me sick.

I'm getting back with my ex-boyfriend. The one that you stole me from. I think I'm in love with him. He's everything that you're not. He has manners, he is considerate, he is smart and he has become a dentist.

I would like to spend some time with him alone. I think I might have a future with him.

I'm moving out of the country for a while. He is moving to the West Bank to volunteer his dental services to Palestinians and I'm going with him. He is so passionate—unlike you.

I think the change is good for me. The kids are yours for now till I return. I'll contact you later to finish the process.

I miss my father. Thanks to you, I won't be able to share the good news with him.

I hate you.

Your soon-to-be ex-wife

PS. I've taken all the money out of the checking and savings accounts. Hope you don't mind. And if you do, I don't care.

I was crushed. This is every man's nightmare: coming home one day and finding your house empty and your wife gone with another man and all your assets. I can not say that I was surprised to see her leave. Even though you think you're ready, you really are not. The feeling of defeat and failure is overwhelming.

Knowing her immense dissatisfaction with me, I often imagined her walking out of my life. I imagined what it would be like to start all over. But you don't really feel the pain until the dagger rips through your heart. It was a confusing time. I was happy that she was gone but sad at the same time. How can you possibly feel two completely different emotions at the same precise moment? How can you love and hate somebody at the same time? How can you be happy and sad when they're not with you anymore? Love is confusing.

The thought of her spending my money with the preppy former ex-boyfriend was devastating. The former ex-boyfriend got his ultimate revenge and finally took back what I stole from him. If I could get my hands on him, I would thank him first for taking my wife and then I would beat the crap out of him for taking my money.

I had to rethink the situation; let's see: I didn't have to see my wife's family anymore or go out of my way to make her happy in bed. I didn't have to always watch what I did around her, always be careful about what I said, and always worry about my family and her family's hostility!

Logically, this should be the best day of my life. But if I was a logical person, I wouldn't be in this mess to begin with.

I called the kids over. I needed to break the news of their mother's disappearance very carefully. I needed to be gentle and sensitive and make sure that they wouldn't be devastated to hear of their beloved mother's desertion. This was an extremely delicate matter that needed to be handled cautiously. But since I never had any training in breaking bad news to my kids or was ever good at beating around the bush, I decided to tell them like it was:

"Hey, kids, I have good news and I have bad news: the good news is your mother has left us; the bad news is we don't have dinner tonight."

Children can always sense when there are problems between their parents. My kids were no exception, but like me, they didn't expect their mother to just take off without saying a word.

"What did you do to her?" my daughter asked while crying.

"How could she do that to us?" my son yelled.

"Why couldn't you be nice to her? Huh?" my daughter said.

"Why did she leave without even saying goodbye?" my son asked.

"Why is this happening to us?" my daughter asked.

"Why is she doing this to us?" my son cried out.

These are difficult times for any parent because we're as helpless as our children when it comes to dealing with separations. We parents are supposed to have all the answers, right? Well, I certainly had no answers for their questions, at least none that they could comprehend.

"It's not what I did to her, but what we did to each other," I answered. "No matter what I say, you will not understand why she's gone and there is nothing I can do to stop your pain."

The kids were confused, devastated, angry and shaken up by the news. The day their mother left was the first day of my children's downfall. I knew from that day on, my kids would not grow up normal and this experience would haunt them in different forms and shapes for the rest of their days.

Children are the true victims of their parents' stupidity. I believe that only a small portion of the world's population is bright enough to be good parents. The rest of us are nothing but a bunch of overgrown wannabes with a license to have children and ruin their lives. Of course, we all think we can be good parents. "Dude, I'll be a good dad. I just know it. It's, like, I just know I'm gonna be a good dad 'cause I love my kids."

We think that just because we love our kids, that automatically make us good parents. Love is no substitute for IQ, and I'm a living testament to that. You want to serve your country? Forget joining the army, get a vasectomy.

I wish there were a law that would force all divorced parents, including myself and the ex, to line up on a football field, get down on their hands and knees, and let their children kick them in the ass for fifteen minutes straight. A weekly event on Sundays during halftimes of every football game, broadcast live into every American's household. And during the Super Bowl, children who're really screwed up by their brainless parents could shoot their parents in the ass with a 12-guage shotgun. They could call it "Super Bowl halftime show sponsored by the NRA." Imagine the ratings.

I was helplessly incapable of easing my children's pain, and I felt like giving each of them a baseball bat, standing in middle of the living room and telling them, "I'm an idiot. Think of me as human piñata; go at it and enjoy."

The wife and her activist former ex-boyfriend moved to Palestine and settled in the West Bank. He rented a place and set up a dental practice to help disadvantaged Palestinians. I guess good dental hygiene was high priority in the war zone.

The arrival of a young Middle Eastern-American dentist and his beautiful girlfriend to help with the cause was big news in the occupied territory. My wife and her former ex-boyfriend became instant celebrities in the West Bank. But after a few months, they became old news and reality started to set in.

The practice was slow, the place was dangerous, the nightlife sucked and the wife started to consider that maybe this was not such a hot idea after all. It didn't take long before she began bitching at the former ex-boyfriend at a hundred miles per hour. The poor guy was trying hard to satisfy her in bed, but the constant bombing and street fighting had taken the thunder out of his down under.

The former ex-boyfriend was exhausted all the time and could not provide quality customer service to his patients. That, in effect, jeopardized the Palestinian uprising, since the young fighters could not fight Israelis with painfully swollen gums and partially pulled out wisdom teeth.

The former ex-boyfriend came under severe scrutiny by the Palestinian authorities for his shabby workmanship. At the same time, my wife found herself living in a house with no running water or electricity. She shared the bathroom with other families in the building and had practically no privacy. The boyfriend was set on experiencing the real living conditions in the occupied territory.

It didn't take my wife long to realize that it's much easier to protect the displaced in the comfort of her living room than by actually being there in person. She began to miss her weekly massage, frequent spa visits, yoga classes, shopping at Neiman Marcus, hanging out at coffee shops with her girlfriends, chilling at home with a glass of wine, etc.

Fighting for a cause, whatever it might be, requires commitment and selflessness. One has to be willing to leave all comforts of everyday industrialized life behind and experience severe pain and suffering. Urban yuppies who act on their ideological impulses often find themselves in an awkward position. My wife and her new man began to realize that political ideals can cause great distress, and it's easier to talk the talk than to fight the fight.

The former ex-boyfriend was also under pressure from Hamas to become a suicide bomber. Since he was a respected dentist with an American passport, the leaders of Hamas believed that it would be easy for him to penetrate deep into Israel and blow himself up. It's true that the dentist was devoted to the Palestinian cause, but the man was not stupid, and his loyalty was there as long as it did not involve any bodily harm. Besides, he was not a type of person that would kill innocent women and children.

The boyfriend also knew that Hamas is not an organization that he could say no to. So he came up with all kind of excuses not to blow himself up. He asked to see suicide bomber's retirement, 401k, worker's compensation, short-term disability and pension plans. He then called in sick every time he was asked to blow himself up:

"Sorry, boss, got a bad flu; how about next Tuesday?"

He told Hamas that he was currently negotiating with Hezbollah's suicide bombing squad and would get back to them after he got his final offer in writing. He also suggested that maybe, instead of blowing himself up, he would be more useful providing free dental checkups for suicide bombers. That was preposterous since the majority of suicide bombers didn't care much about their dental conditions, considering what would be left of their teeth after they were done.

The Hamas organization finally gave up on my wife's former ex-boyfriend, concluding that the dentist dude was not as devoted to the Palestinian cause as originally believed. Nevertheless, Hamas decided to punish the dentist and send a clear message to all the gutless wannabes out there who wanted to use the Palestinian cause to satisfy their own sense of charity. But when Hamas' enforcers heard stories from the neighbors about the dentist being nagged to death by my wife, they concluded that the dentist was being punished enough and left him alone.

My wife's bitch meter was running on turbocharged and she made the boyfriend's life a living hell. So much that one day, according to live witness accounts, the pitiable dentist left his office in the West Bank and jumped in front of an Israeli tank just to take his own life.

"I saw him come out of his office," a witness said to the news crew. "He looked dazed. A long line of Israeli tanks were passing through the street. He took off all his clothes and yelled, 'Say hello to my little friend.' He then jumped in front of a tank."

"Just like that?" the reporter asked.

"Yeah, pretty much."

I understood the feeling. I myself felt like jumping in front of a tank or two from time to time so that I wouldn't hear my wife's constant complaining. You might ask why I married her if she was such a difficult person. The answer is simple: she was sweet when I met her, but years of living with me had turned her into an unbearable personality, and I take full responsibility for that.

She was a woman of substance and potential who chose to marry a man of no such qualities. And one day she realized that she had wasted her life and by then she was older, had two kids, no skills and no self-esteem. That alone would make anybody bitter.

My wife returned from the West Bank and moved back in with her family. It didn't take her long to find another boyfriend, file for divorce, and take custody of the kids.

It was a difficult period of my life. Life was hell without my kids around. I was going crazy. Even though my kids were two out-of-control lunatics, they were my lunatics and I loved them to death. I fell into a deep depression. I also missed my wife. I couldn't stand being around her for a second but still there was something there. I felt like chasing the American dream had knocked me on my rear end, and the Woman upstairs hadn't been kind. I basically had no appetite for other people's pains and miseries. I had enough of my own.

I had reached my limit of social tolerance and preferred to stay away from people as much as I possibly could; I sincerely couldn't stand people. My attention span was nowhere to be found, and sarcasm became an effective means of communication. I listened to people talk, and all I could hear was the sound of the wind generated by the flapping of their mouths.

My ex-wife called one day. She wanted me to sign more papers prepared by her lawyers to finalize the divorce. I didn't care anymore. I didn't even ask; just bring it on. She gave me her typical attitude of indifference followed by rash of guilt trip. The woman had taken my kids, my house, my car, my savings accounts and everything else, and she still managed to make me feel guilty.

She wanted me to meet her at this trendy coffee shop on New York's Fifth Avenue to sign the papers. This is the place where Middle Eastern Generation Xers get together once a month and read poetry. Then they talk about their cultural mishaps and confusing lives as Middle Eastern-Americans. Girls bitch about their families not letting them experiment with sex and drugs or date Puerto Ricans, and guys talk about their confusing ideals and cultural clashes with their American girlfriends. Big frickin' deal. Get a life.

I got myself some Paxils and washed them down with three shots of vodka. I took the subway to Third Avenue, walked two blocks down, and entered the coffee shop. You couldn't help noticing the BMWs parked up front. The Iranians were in the house. The coffee shop was packed with people.

I elbowed my way to the back where I found my ex-wife sitting at a table, listening to some skinny guy reading a poem. I looked at the guy more closely and realized that he must be her new boyfriend. He matched the profile, based on what my kids had described. My kids told me that their mother's new boyfriend was a "skinny poet therapist" or something like that.

He was reciting his poem in Farsi, but every time he ran out of rhyme, he used an English word. My ex-wife was looking at the dork with the most adoring look on her face. She didn't even notice me standing in front of her. That bothered me. She used to notice me and now I was invisible to her.

I listened to the poem for a few minutes. I was burning with jealousy and rage. The thought of this little midget scoring with my wife was killing me. How could she prefer this moving skeleton over me? What did this pencil-neck have that I didn't?

I had to do something. I laughed out laud and said, "Hafez is turning in his grave."

Everyone in the room turned around and looked at me with their eyes wide open. My ex shook her head and said, "I should have known better than to ask you to come here."

The ex-wife's new boyfriend stared at me for a minute and said, "How ironic. Now this is what I was talking about in my poem. Persian baby boomers that refuse to accept change and modify their ways."

"First of all," I said, "I'm not Persian. I'm Iranian and I'm still looking for a country called Persia on the map. I'm not a baby and the only thing booming are my hemorrhoids. I'll tell you what's ironic. It's my ex-wife sitting here and listening to your crap while my children are being looked after by a stranger called the babysitter."

The poet stood up, looked at the crowd and said, "Ladies and gentlemen, this is a prime example of a forty-something Persian man who has difficulties adjusting to his environment. This man still thinks his ex-wife is his maid, and even though she's not his wife anymore, he has problems accepting the fact that she's with someone else. As a Ph.D. in psychology from UCLA, I call this PMS or Persian Male Syndrome."

The poet looked at me and continued, "My friend, you are in America. Women here are not life-long properties of their husbands. You need to let go. 'Not without my daughter' is passé." He got a standing ovation from the crowd.

I looked at my ex-wife. She was jumping up and down, clapping, and blowing kisses at the poet. I felt like my head was about to explode. How the hell did the guy know that I considered the ex-wife my life-long property? How did he know that I had problems letting go of her? The bastard was good!

I waited until the crowd was calm and quiet. I walked slowly towards her new boyfriend. I stopped five feet away from him. "You are wrong," I calmly said. "What you have here is not a forty-something Persian man who's got PMS. What you got yourself here is a forty-something Iranian man who's going to kick your ass."

I ran and jumped on him like a wounded animal. I landed a head butt right in his nose, followed by an uppercut. The "poet therapist" made a weak buzzing sound and passed out. All of a sudden, all hell broke loose and everybody was on top of me. The crowd pulled me off the poet who was horizontally motionless.

A few more punches and kicks were exchanged between me and the angry crowd. The Generation Xers could fight. I was surprised. But they underestimated the shamelessness of a man who has nothing to lose.

The fight eventually moved to the street. A few pedestrians and bystanders joined in and it became a full-blown rumble. Everybody was punching everybody else. People were bumping into BMWs and setting off security alarms. The owners were running around screaming, trying to push people off their cars.

Then I spotted my ex-wife's boyfriend. The little weasel was trying to sneak out of the coffee shop. I ran and tackled him from behind. We both hit the pavement hard. I got on top of him. I grabbed his hair with one hand and slapped him on the face a few times. With each slap, I shouted, "This one is for sleeping with my ex-wife. This one is for telling my kids to call you Daddy. This one is for driving my car. This one is for spending my money—"

My ex-wife and a couple of other guys pulled me off the poet. The poor guy was knocked out again. My ex-wife started screaming at me. "Have you gone mad? What the hell is your problem?"

"Tell the asshole that my children are off limits. Get it? They only have one father and that's me. Tell him."

"Tell who?"

"Your freaking boyfriend," I said, pointing at the semiconscious poet.

"What are you talking about? I had never seen this man until tonight."

"What? Isn't he your 'poet therapist' boyfriend?"

"Poet therapist? My boyfriend is out of town, and he is a podiatrist, not a poet therapist."

"But the kids told me he was a poet therapist."

"Because the kids can't pronounce podiatrist, you moron."

"Are you sure he's not your boyfriend?"

"Yes, I'm sure."

"So, who is he?" I said.

"Who is he?" my ex-wife said. "He is a Pulitzer-prize-winning writer and poet. He is also one of the most renowned psychologists with tons of books on human behavior; if you ever read a book, you might know him."

"No kidding, is he, like, famous?"

"Yes."

"You don't suppose I can get his autograph?" I asked.

"Why don't you ask him when comes out of the coma," my ex-wife said.

This was not good. I, again, let my pride and paranoia get the best of me. I beat up a man who had nothing to do with my messed-up life. I made a monster out of him, blamed all my problems on him, and punished him for my own inadequacies. And the worst part is that the man is an icon. What was I thinking? I felt bad about this incident. Why don't I use my brain? Why do I always let emotions dictate the course of actions in my life?

Well, I was at fault and I had to do the right thing. I had to do what every decent human being in my shoes would do. It was about time for me to stand up for once and take responsibility for my actions. There was only one thing to do. So, I looked left, I looked right and I ran for my life.

7. *El Cheapo* Got Me into Trouble

REZA IS A SHREWD IRANIAN-AMERICAN BUSINESSMAN who prides himself on being the biggest charlatan in North America. He is the type who paints a Yugo and sells it as a Cadillac. He cheats, lies, deceives and manipulates with ease and sleeps like a baby at night. Reza, the only son of a multimillionaire businessman from the city of Mashhad, should be the poster child for Planned Parenthood. They should hang a picture of him on the wall with these words, "Here is another reason for birth control."

He is an equal-opportunity swindler who has no mercy on anyone, even his own family. He defrauded his brother-in-law on a real estate deal which resulted in his in-law's bankruptcy. In a nutshell, Reza is one mean, lying, cheating, shish kabob-eating machine, who has no respect for human dignity and no sense of business integrity.

You might wonder why I know so much about him. Well, he's my cousin, *El Cheapo*.

My cousin Reza has no friends and he calls me only when he needs something. Although he has millions of dollars in the bank, he never pays for lunch, and he always leaves his wallet at home. He drives a cheap car and lives in a one-bedroom apartment.

When *El Cheapo* shows up at my house, my kids run to their rooms and lock their doors. My kids don't want to have anything to do with Reza since he constantly asks to borrow money from them. Imagine a thirty-five-year-old millionaire asking two teens to lend him money.

"Dad, your cousin is a jackass."

"I know, honey."

He normally comes to visit me for two reasons: one is to finish all the food and beers in my refrigerator, and two is to get online and surf porn sites on my computer.

Reza came to my house one day to share a revelation. I warned him I wasn't interested in hearing about his latest swindle. He assured me it was a personal matter. Reza is a private person who hardly ever shares his personal life with his family. So I was a bit curious and mildly interested.

"This place didn't feel like home for the longest time," Reza said. "Different culture, language, looks. I always thought—someday—I would go back home and stay. But the more I stay here, the more I get used to it. So I made up my mind. I am going to start a family here. It's time, you know."

"I'm happy for you. So I guess it's time to go to back to the Middle East and bring back a bride?"

"Actually, I don't need to go back home," Reza said. "There is this girl here that I met a little while ago. She's perfect for me. She has the same family values, stature and mentality as I do. She's traditional, religious and upright. She can cook, clean, take care of the house, do the laundry—did I mention clean?"

"So you want a maid."

"I want a wife. Someone I can have kids with," Reza responded.

"So you want a maid you can have sex with."

"Whatever. I have to meet her father to ask permission for his daughter's hand in marriage. I need a wingman, a comrade, a sidekick; someone who can give me courage, someone who will pick me up when I stumble. I need you to go with me."

I stepped back. "Hell, no."

"Please, I am desperate," *El Cheapo* said. "I can't do this alone. Nobody in the family talks to me except you. I have no friends. This is my future we are talking here. I'll do all the talking, and you won't have to say a word. I promise."

"No way."

"You're my blood. You're the only thing I have. How can you say no to me?"

"Read my lips: nooooooo."

"I'll give you a thousand dollars."

"Two thousand."

"Fifteen hundred and a Persian rug."

"You're on," I replied.

Reza picked me up the next day. He was uptight and visibly nervous. He didn't say much. We drove to the nicer part of the town where all the rich people live. He stopped the car by a huge house. We walked to the door and rang the bell. Reza's face looked lifeless. A short, bald, middle-aged man opened the door. He had long green prayer beads in his left hand. He asked us to take off our shoes and walk in. He was the father of the bride.

Inside the house was drastically different from the outside. There were mirrors stuck to the ceiling and the walls. There was no furniture anywhere; however, there were tons of oversized Persian rugs on the floor. We walked to a huge living room, which was completely empty, and sat on the floor. There were a number of young women in the house. Some of the girls served us tea, candies, and fruit. They were playfully giggling and laughing.

Reza was sitting down motionless. He looked like a zombie. I was waiting for him to start the introduction, but nothing came out of his mouth. I kept looking at him, but he looked dazed and confused. Things were getting awkward. There was a long silence. I figured if I start talking, Reza might come out of the coma and take over.

"Well, sir, my cousin, Reza, is here to ask your permission to marry your daughter. Reza is a man of integrity, wisdom, values and virtues." I felt my nose growing.

"Which daughter?" the father of the bride asked.

I looked at Reza with anticipation. Reza looked as if he was dead—he was in la-la land. He was looking through the window at some infinite point with no apparent sign of life.

"Pardon?" I exclaimed.

"Which daughter? I have seven daughters. Which one do you have in mind?" the man patiently asked.

I looked at Reza again. He was sleeping with his eyes open. He looked as if he was meditating. I wanted to kill the jerk. He was embarrassing me. I felt like getting up and kicking him in the balls.

The father of the bride looked calm. He paused for a minute and said, "Well, regardless of which daughter, here are my terms: There will be an alimony contract that would include five hundred thousand dollars cash, a house, SUV, appropriate gifts, jewelry and all the furniture. She will walk into her husband's house with a holy Koran, clothes on her back and her charm. I congratulate your cousin and wish them both a good life and prosperity."

All of the sudden, *El Cheapo* came back to life. He jumped up like a wild animal and said, "Do you think I'm stupid? Five hundred thousand dollars, a car and a house? I am not marrying the queen of England you know. You've got to be joking. Here is what I got for you, old man: Two installments of a hundred thousand dollars and maybe a compact car for her alimony. Your daughter's dowry should include two sets of furniture, plasma TV, washer, dryer, kitchen appliances and at least twenty Persian rugs."

Reza paused and looked at me. "Make that twenty-one Persian rugs."

The father of the bride looked stunned. He just realized that he wasn't dealing with an average man but the devil himself. *El Cheapo* has spoken.

"Young man, I'm not that rich to accommodate my daughter with such an elaborate dowry," the man said.

"Bullshit. I've done a background check on you," Reza said. "I know exactly how much you are worth; don't even go there."

The man paused for a second. "Okay, how about a lump sum of three hundred and fifty thousand dollars and the house for alimony, and my daughter will bring with her five Persian rugs and a big-screen TV."

Reza looked at me while shaking his head and said, "Do I look stupid? Do I have an 'I am the village idiot' sign on my forehead? Am I not making myself clear?"

I couldn't believe this. What the hell were these guys doing? They sounded like they were trading camels. I was speechless. Is this normal? Am I missing something here? Do people do this nowadays? What should I do?

The father of the bride played with his prayer beads. He shifted his weight and calmly said, "Agha joon (dear sir), I was born at night but not last night. You can't possibly think I would give my daughter away to a guy like you who is two Prozacs short of a mental hospital. You can never find girls as virtuous as my daughters. Nobody has touched these girls, and as God is my witness, nobody will but their husbands. My seven daughters wear chastity belts and I'm the only man who holds the keys and I will personally deliver the keys to their husbands."

Did I hear him say, "chastity belts?" Was he speaking metaphorically or do his daughters really wear them? What happens when he is not around and they need to use the lavatory? What if he misplaces the keys? What if his daughters secretly date locksmiths? That would defeat the purpose, don't you think? What if his daughters decide to go swimming? Wouldn't they sink right to the bottom?

Reza thought for a second and said, "Two installments of hundred and twenty thousand dollars and a sports car; in return you will pay for the wedding and she will bring in five Persian rugs of my choice plus a refrigerator, bedroom set, and a big-screen TV. That's my final offer and it's nonnegotiable." Reza stood up, looked at me like I was his butler and said, "Get up. We're out of here."

I jumped up and followed him. Reza stopped on the way out and looked at a framed miniature painting hanging on the wall.

He turned around, looked at the man and said, "I'll leave you my phone number. Consider my offer and call me if you change your mind. By the way, I want you to throw in this frame as a gesture of goodwill."

I pulled the man aside and asked, "Pardon me, did you say 'chastity belt?' Where do you get one? I'm thinking about getting one for my daughter. Where can I find one?"

"Try eBay," the man said.

We walked out of the house and sat in the car. I looked at Reza and asked, "So, what the hell just happened?"

"Nothing; he'll come around. He has seven daughters. Do you have any idea how expensive it is to have seven daughters? He has no leverage for negotiation. For all he's asking, I might as well marry his youngest daughter."

"You're sick—she's only fourteen."

"She'll grow up."

Well, Reza was correct in his assessment. The father of the bride did come around and eventually agreed with the devil's terms and conditions. The wedding was on, and Reza was successful in sealing yet another lucrative deal.

Since his future father-in-law was paying for the wedding, Reza spared no expense. He booked a prime spot on a golf course and invited everybody with whom he had ever come into contact. Since the overwhelming majority of people who knew Reza wanted to kill him, only a few accepted his invitation. But that was no problem since his future wife's family had plenty of acquaintances and could easily fill up the entire place.

My work was done. I stayed low key throughout the wedding planning. I didn't want to get involved with anything that had anything to do with Reza and his wedding. I told him that from now on he was on his own.

I didn't hear from Reza for a month until one day I heard a message on my answering machine: Reza was asking me for a big favor. My first reaction was, no way in hell.

I didn't return his call but the bastard was persistent. I finally called him back. "What?"

"I need a big favor from you."

"No," I replied.

"Oh, please. It's really nothing," he said.

"Then do it yourself."

"I can't. I have no time. I'm busy with the wedding plans. Please, I really need you to do this for me," he said.

"What is it?"

"I need you to go to this address and pick up the wedding cake."

That wasn't too bad. I could do that for him. After all, he was family.

"I guess."

"You're the man," Reza said. "Listen, this is very important. This cake is specially ordered by the future wife, and you have to go to this Middle Eastern lady's apartment to pick it up. She makes the cake from unique ingredients and spices which are imported from India. It cost the future father-in-law seven thousand dollars to have it made. Whatever you do, get it to the wedding reception on time."

"Fine."

"Listen, the future wife is going gaga over this cake. Whatever you do, don't screw it up."

"Shut up before I change my mind," I said.

"Okay, thanks."

On the day of the wedding, I took the van and drove to the address that Reza had given to me. I double-parked the van and ran upstairs to apartment 302. I knocked on the door. An old Middle Eastern lady opened the door and let me in.

There were a bunch of young Middle Eastern men sitting on the couch watching MTV. She told me to go to the kitchen and wait there. I did as directed.

There it was. The cake was absolutely magnificent. Five tiers of delight. She must have spent two weeks working on that cake. I tried to dip my finger in and have a little early sample of the cake, but the old lady came from nowhere and smacked my hand before I could reach it. That hurt.

I stood there and watched with admiration as the old lady disassembled the cake and put it inside boxes. She closed the boxes and wrapped them with ribbons.

All of a sudden, the door to the apartment blew to pieces, and a group of armed men in commando outfits stormed the apartment. Guns up and ready, they rushed to the kitchen and took me down to the floor. Before I knew what was happening, I was handcuffed and pinned down. Honestly, I shit my pants.

The apartment was filled with smoke and tear gas. I couldn't see a thing. There were yelling and shouting while people scrambled around the apartment in frenzy. I thought I was going to die.

The commandos picked me up, covered my head with a bag, carried me downstairs and threw me inside a vehicle. I was speechless. What the hell was going on?

About an hour later, the bag was removed from my head and I found myself in a police interrogation room surrounded by three big men in cheap suits. The men were looking at me like I was an alien from Mars. I could see my reflection in a two-way mirror directly in front of me. I looked horrifying.

"What the hell is going on here?" I screamed.

"Shut up, you goddamn terrorist."

"What?"

"Who are your contacts? Where were you taking the bomb?" the agent said.

"The bomb? What bomb?" I asked.

"Don't play games. We know everything. Where were you taking it?"

"Taking what?"

"The bomb."

"What bomb?" I asked.

"Listen, you asshole, I'll have you shipped to Guantanamo before you know it. I'll have your ass in there till you turn seventy."

"I want my lawyer."

"Lawyer? You don't get no freakin' lawyer. Al-Quaida gets no lawyers, you scumbag."

"Al-Quaida? What the hell are you talking about?" I asked.

"You know what I'm talking about. You were supposed to pick up the bomb and deliver it to your Al-Quaida contacts. Who are they? I want names."

"What bomb? I was picking up a cake," I said.

"There were dirty bombs in those boxes. Where were you takin' 'em?"

"It's a cake. I was picking up a cake for my cousin's wedding."

"Shut up. We know it's a dirty bomb; we know everything about you. Who are your contacts? What were you going to blow up? Where is Osama?"

"What the hell are you talking about?"

"Give me some names and make things easier for yourself. Who are your Al-Quaida buddies? Where are your safe houses?"

"It was a cake. I swear. It was a wedding cake. I was sent by my cousin to pickup his wedding cake," I said.

"So your cousin is an operative. Who is he? Did he meet with Osama before coming here?"

"My cousin can't even tie his own shoes. Are you people crazy?"

"Well, we sent the boxes to the crime lab. We'll have the results back in a few minutes, and when they tell me it's a bomb, your ass is mine."

"It's a cake," I said.

"Shut up."

"Wait, I know, my ex-wife put you up to this. This is a joke, right?"

"It's as real as it can get, you stupid towel-head."

"What are you gonna do to me?" I asked.

The agent gave me the universal symbol for "I'll-slash-your-throat" and smiled. I couldn't believe this was happening to me.

Like millions of Middle Eastern-American folks, my life was turned upside down on September 11th. I couldn't comprehend how a group of Middle Eastern men could commit such horrendous crimes. Why would you want to kill innocent people like that? It just didn't make any sense to me.

I've lived most of my life in the United States and I love this country. And like the majority of Middle Eastern folks in the U.S., I believe in what this country stands for. I believe in freedom, democracy and human rights. I love America because, unlike where I came from, I press forward in life based on what I know, not who I know. I love America because nobody tells me and my children what to do, what to wear, how to look, how to think, what to eat, what music to listen to, what book to read, what politics to believe in and what religion to practice. I love America because I'm not above the law and neither is the chump sitting next to me. And most importantly, I love America because she lets me be. It's true that the system is not perfect, but it's better than what I'm used to.

I like to form my own opinion about subject matter, and I don't give a crap what Osama or the ayatollah says about America; I know what I know and I don't allow others to think for me. It doesn't matter who you are. The moment you entitle yourself to present your stupid ideology on my behalf, you automatically appear on my shit list.

And no, you're not the representative of God on earth, you will not go to Heaven by blowing yourself up and killing innocent women and children and there are no virgins up there waiting for you. Get a life. If Heaven is roamed by people like the hijackers who blew up the twin towers, then send me to hell because there will be some serious problems in Heaven when I run into those guys on the way to claiming my virgins.

Yeah, I might not agree with every foreign or domestic policy decision that the administration makes, but I'm a sane human being and I'll not harm innocent people to make political statements. You know what I do? I vote. And I have not found a single verse in the Koran that says kill innocent women and children for Allah. There is a better way: it's called lobbying.

Having said that, I couldn't believe I was being accused of being a terrorist. What happened to my rights? How can this happen in America?

There was a long and deadly silence in the room. All three agents were staring at me. I was staring in disbelief at my own reflection in the two-way mirror. This was not a very comfortable situation. Sweat dripped down my forehead and I needed to pee.

The phone rang. One of the agents answered the phone. "Uha-uha-uha. Are you sure? Uha-uha. Okay, thanks."

He hung up the phone and rushed outside. The other two agents followed him in a hurry.

This was creepy. I was sure that I was dead. Speaking of being in the wrong place at the wrong time. I could've killed Reza. Just give me five minutes with him. If I ever see him again, his ass is mine. But then again, they're sending me to Guantanamo. I won't see anybody anymore—my kids, my parents, my friends. I could picture myself lying naked on the ground attached to a leash with a prison guard babe holding the other end. I personally wouldn't mind that in the privacy of my bedroom but not in a prison. This is a nightmare.

The door to the room swung open and the three agents walked back in. They had a very tame look on their faces. The agent who originally interrogated me spoke, "We just got the results back from the crime lab."

I gasped for air.

"You were correct. It was a cake."

The three agents looked down at the floor. "As a matter of fact, we raided the wrong apartment," the agent said. "We were supposed to raid apartment two-oh-two not three-oh-two. You know how it is, the boys got excited, went into the wrong apartment, what can you do? No hard feelings, I hope."

"Where is my cake?" I asked.

"Well, we used some of it for testing and the boys at the lab ate the rest. They said it was quite tasty."

"What? You guys ate my cake?"

"Sorry, we'll drop you off at a grocery store. You can buy a new one. Uncle Sam will pick up the tab."

"Wait, you don't understand. I have to have that cake. That wasn't just any cake, it was made of special spices imported from India," I said.

"Sorry."

"My cousin's wife is gonna kill me," I said.

"Sorry."

"Do you know any word other than 'sorry'?"

"Nope, sorry."

Reza's wedding was over by the time my paperwork was completed and I was released. I drove home after midnight and crashed in my bed. It was good to be home.

I checked my answering machine the next day and found Reza's message from the night before, which consisted of a collection of tasteless words followed by an assortment of insults. Reza never called me back after that. This experience worked out better than I expected.

8. The Kids Are Yours

MEANWHILE, THINGS WERE NOT SO HOT between my ex-wife and her podiatrist boyfriend. The guy didn't like the fact that the kids were always around. The lover boy felt that he didn't have enough privacy. I guess somebody forgot to tell him he was dating a woman with two kids, for God's sake.

I, on the other hand, manipulated the kids to make my ex-wife and her boyfriend's life a living hell by constantly causing trouble. The kids loved it, and I enjoyed seeing the boyfriend hating his life and feeling trapped in a nightmarish relationship with a bitchy single mother and two crazy delinquents. Oh, the joy.

Like many hot-blooded Middle Eastern men, I blamed all my problems and faults on other people. It's easier that way. You don't have to do much when you convince yourself that your lack of ingenuity, resourcefulness, and success is due to other people's malicious interventions in your daily life. That way you are not required to take responsibility for your own actions, and you certainly don't have to go through the trouble of correcting your mistakes.

Ask any Middle Eastern man why things are so messed up back home and he will tell you stories about all kinds of conspiracy theories and elaborate plans by foreign forces to keep us down. You never hear a Middle Eastern man say, "Hey, dude, thing are messed up back home 'cause it's easier to blame shit on other people than get up early in the morning and work twelve-hour-days. The hell with that."

I, too, blamed my messed up life on my ex-wife's boyfriend. The thought of this guy making a home with my ex-wife and my kids was killing me. I'm a brainless but proud man who loves his family, and nobody shall enjoy the fruits of my labor other than me. I would use anything in my command to stop that. So I did everything in my power to make sure that the podiatrist was unhappy with my ex-wife and the kids.

Am I a sick man? Yes, I am. Do I need professional help? Yes, I do. Should they lock me up in a mental hospital and throw away the key? Yes, they should. What can I say? I'm a guy, and like any other chap out there, I don't like other men touching my stuff.

When the kids stayed with me, we spent quality time coming up with elaborate plans to completely ruin my ex-wife and her boyfriend's relationship. Oh, we had so much fun. It was educational, and it brought me and the kids closer together than ever. I increased the kids' allowances (effective form of bribery) and spoiled the crap out of them. At the same time, I put ideas in their heads: "Wouldn't it be fun if you guys played loud rap music in your rooms all day while staying at home with your mom? Hey, I would let you do it."

"Mom doesn't let us listen to rap, Dad."

"Oh, just do it. She'll love it, I guarantee it."

At first the boyfriend tried to establish a communication channel with the kids. Being an educated man, he believed that all problems can be resolved by communicating your feelings in a civilized manner. But the only channel of communication the kids wanted to have was with their friends through their cell phones.

The boyfriend gave up on the communication thing and tried to be a father figure for the kids. He believed that the kids were acting stupid because they were missing the presence of a full-time father in their lives. That blew up in his face since my kids didn't even respect their own biological father, let alone respecting him, a stranger, as a father figure.

He then tried to engage the kids in science and academic projects. Having inherited my genes, the kids had no interest whatsoever in science or anything that required thinking. You gave the kids some food and a couple of video games, and they were happy.

The boyfriend tried everything short of bribery to get close to the kids but nothing worked. He finally came to the conclusion that he was unable to make the necessary connection with them and he couldn't stand them anymore. Do you blame him? Heck, I'm their father and even I sometimes can't stand them.

My plans were simple yet effective. I would feed the kids cereal, candies, cookies, and chocolate with massive amount of Red Bull before dropping them off at their mother's house. The kids were so wired on sugar and caffeine that they would destroy their mother's house in a matter of minutes. They would run around the house like "JoJo, the Indian circus boy," and jump like loaded springs, crashing into furniture, breaking everything in their path.

I would let them stay up all night playing video games, which would affect their sleeping habits. They were dead tired by the time they went back to their mother's house. That made it challenging for my ex-wife and the boyfriend to get the kids up on time and ready for school.

I would show them scary movies night after night. The poor kids would have nightmares for weeks, and they would run into their mother's bedroom, keeping the ex-wife and her boyfriend up all night.

But the worst thing I did, which I'm not very proud of, was to get the podiatrist into trouble by infiltrating one of his intellectual gatherings.

You see, the boyfriend was a very cultured man with many boring hobbies like reading and writing. He was involved with scientific societies and literary clubs. He held a book club meeting in his house once a month and invited his nerdy male colleagues to join him for tea and a discussion of the latest books on the market. How boring can you get?

Meanwhile, my ex-wife would leave the house and go visit her family while the meeting was in progress, and she would return just before the book club meeting was about to wrap up. I gathered all this information from my kids.

I hired two strippers and sent them to the book club meeting. The aim was to have my wife walk in while the strippers were performing their magic. Knowing how much my wife despised the whole stripper act, I figured the boyfriend would be history.

Knowing exactly what time my wife was coming home, I personally drove the strippers to the boyfriend's house and paid them in full, including some extra cash for added enthusiasm. I told the strippers that they were walking into a sex addicts and fetishists' anonymous meeting. I also told the strippers that these guys were old pros who liked to play games, and they might look reluctant at first but what they really wanted was ultimate nuttiness and fulfillment of their dirtiest fantasies. The strippers were drugged up and didn't even care.

"Yeah, whatever."

The strippers let themselves into the house, turned on their boom box and started going at it in front of the book club. The entire book club watched the lesbian/instrumental act with disbelief. Some of the old geezers hadn't seen naked women in years. The book club folks felt movement in a part of their bodies that had not had a pulse in years. This was going to be a book club meeting to remember.

The nerdy boys, starving for bit of action, started to get jiggy with it, and the meeting turned to a full-blown bash. The book club began dancing, stripping and busting out with dollar bills. Watson, hold your hat; it's a party!

Meanwhile the baffled boyfriend tried to push the strippers out of his house. He justly panicked, knowing that my ex-wife could be home any minute, and if she saw the strippers, there would be severe repercussions. The strippers thought that the boyfriend was acting out one of his fantasies, so they put it in overdrive, doing what strippers do. At the same time, the book club threatened to inflict bodily harm on the boyfriend if he didn't shut up and get out of the way. Seeing that the book club cavalry was about to attack, the boyfriend backed off and stayed quiet.

It was loud, hot, heavy, sweaty, and there was lots of grinding going on. Books were flying all over the room. The boys were excited beyond imagination.

The ex-wife walked in. The boyfriend froze. One of the new book club boys, thinking that my ex-wife was another stripper joining the party late, ran over and started grinding and rubbing against her. Seeing fresh meat, some other book club boys jumped into the mix like vultures and the ex found herself sandwiched between a bunch of horny Neanderthals. The boyfriend ran in between the ex and the guys, attempting to rescue her from the circle of passion.

The book club got sick and tired of the podiatrist's party-pooping attitude and lack of participation. The boys picked up the boyfriend, carried him out of the room, dumped him into the basement and locked the door.

I was watching the whole thing through a window while hiding behind the bushes in the front yard. The ex-wife was running around the room, screaming while being chased by the book club boys; the strippers were busy doing their thing; the music was blasting out of the house. A few of the neighbors came outside to check on the commotion. Some of the book club boys were mooning the neighbors and running around the house in their underwear. This was turning out better than I expected. Heck, the party was so good, I was tempted to get inside and get my groove on.

My plans were working beautifully. The ex-wife and her boyfriend were arguing frequently, and it was all because of my relentless tricks and exploitation of the kids' unruly behavior. It felt great. I was like a puppet master. I would pull the strings and all hell would break loose. My ex-wife's household was in chaos. Life couldn't be better.

Suspicious of my intentions in using the kids and pulling crazy stunts to jeopardize her relationship with the podiatrist, my ex-wife asked me to meet her in person. She was very nice to me on the phone. That scared me. It was apparent that she was on to me. This was going to be ugly. I reluctantly agreed to meet her. I suggested that we meet at a restaurant. I figured I would be safe in a public place in case my ex-wife decided to attack me.

We met at a sandwich shop near my house. She looked good. I was nervous. She sat on a chair across from me and reached inside her handbag. I dove to the floor, thinking that she was pulling out a pistol. It turned out to be a folder. I got back on my chair. She slammed the folder on the table and said, "You win."

"Sorry?"

"They are yours."

"Who?"

"The kids are yours," she said. "I've requested reverse custody. You get the kids during the week and I get them some weekends."

"Sorry?"

"They are yours. You won."

"What do you mean? I can't have the kids. I have no time to be a full-time parent," I said.

"Well, you had time to brainwash them, you had time to come up with elaborate plans to ruin my life, so I'm sure you'll have time to raise them."

"Brainwash? Me? No way."

"Cut the crap. All you have to do is to sign these papers and the kids are yours. Knock yourself out."

"I want the whole package. I want the kids and I want the wife back," I said.

"I'd rather eat poison and die before I get back with you," she said.

"Come on. Am I that horrible?"

"Yes," she said.

Okay, maybe she had a point, but I understood what she was up to. She wanted to give me a taste of my own medicine. She wanted me to deal with the monsters I had created. She was smarter than I thought.

I signed the papers and the kids moved in. That was the biggest mistake of my life. It was a reversal of fortune in the sickest way. The ex-wife became the puppet master and I became the victim of my own misdeeds. The ex-wife returned the favor by manipulating the kids to act stupid when they were with me. My life was hell, and for the first time I realized the consequences of the dangerous games I was playing.

The kids were the byproduct of a broken home and stupid parents, and they were pretty screwed up in the head. And now I was stuck with them. I certainly couldn't blame this one on anybody but myself. It was my own doing, so I sucked it up and took it like a man.

I was outmaneuvered, outplayed and outclassed by the ex-wife, and she got her revenge. But it was okay because I had more tricks up my sleeve. This certainly wasn't the end of it.

9. Hanging Out With the Boy

I WAS SITTING IN THE OFFICE, working on my usual nine-hour daydreaming session, when my boss rudely interrupted me.

"I would like to invite you to my son's party," he said, handing me the invitation.

"Oh, a birthday party?" I asked.

"No. Circumcision party."

What the hell! I almost fell off my chair. I opened the invitation, and sure enough, it was a circumcision party.

Noticing my freaky and uncomfortable reaction, my boss explained, "My wife is from the Middle East, and traditionally, boys are circumcised between the ages of five and twelve. She wanted it that way."

Things like this happen quite often in the Middle East where friends, neighbors and relatives are invited to circumcision parties. Tea, sweets and refreshments are served while the grownups watch the poor kid getting his thingy chopped off. I guess it makes grownups feel good about themselves since they are not the ones on display (for a change), and it's not their equipment that is getting rearranged.

But I never thought people in their right mind would throw a circumcision party nowadays, especially in America. I thought they would take care of the business in the hospital as soon as the kid is born and get it over with. That's what I did with my son, and I was very happy with the results.

Newborn boys are too stupid to realize that half of their manhood is about to be sliced off by a sharp knife. It surely prevents boys from getting traumatized by the act since they won't remember a thing when they grow up. It makes perfect sense because there will be many other episodes in life that will traumatize men, such as marriage and credit card bills.

Come to think of it, circumcising boys later in life is not a bad idea and probably is an effective weapon to control kids' behavior. I wouldn't have had my son circumcised in the hospital if I knew then what I know now. I would've waited until he was older, and then I would use the occasion as threat to get him to do his everyday chores around the house.

"You go clean your room this instant or I'll circumcise your ass."

I would've made a circumcision party invitation card but I wouldn't have mailed it yet. I would've left the date blank, and every time he got out of line, I would wave the card in front of his face and say, "Guess who is having a party?"

Well, I guess that's why I'm not regarded as visionary by friends and family.

Honestly, I was not sure what to expect. I mean, what do you wear to a party like that? Should I go casual or should I wear suit and tie? What do you take to a circumcision party? Flowers, cookies, Band-Aid? What do you do while you are at the party? Are they gonna play music? Is there dinner? Can you take a date? What kind of drinks do they serve? Champagne?

I asked my son to join me in this interesting escapade. It would be a father-son field trip. I wanted him to experience Middle Eastern culture firsthand. And what better way to get in touch with your roots than seeing a little boy getting his willy chopped off.

My son was not very excited about the idea. "Thanks, Dad. Other kids go to the ballpark with their dads, and you're taking me to a circumcision party? You suck, Dad."

"Hey, if I'm gonna suffer, you're gonna suffer with me. That's what family is about; it's all about suffering together."

I pulled into the street where my boss and his family live. I'm one of those Iranians who are always late for parties, but I was not about to be late for this one. I guess I was just curious. I felt sorry for the boy. But I had never been invited to a circumcision party before.

I found a spot, parked my car and walked to the house. My son reluctantly followed me from behind. The door was open and the house was full of people. I got there just in time. The ceremony was about to begin. The poor kid was standing on a table with his pants down, looking confused. There was a circle of people around him, mostly men and some women. There was a skinny guy standing in front of the boy with surgical gloves, scissors and clamps ready to go at it.

"Is he a doctor?" I asked the gentleman next to me.

"He is a used car salesman and a part-time circumcision master. He circumcises Jews and Moslems."

"How good is he?" I asked the man.

"He is so good that I went back to him last year for a touch up."

"What do you mean 'a touch up'?"

"Well, I wasn't very happy with the look. It kind of looked unhappy. It's supposed to look happy, right? So I took it back and he did his magic. I'm very pleased with the results."

"You were unhappy with your circumcision?" I asked.

"Yes, I was, but it looks marvelous now."

"Who cares how it looks?" I said.

"I do. I'm a perfectionist."

This is a prime example of man's obsession with his penis. A man spends more time looking at his penis than any other part of his body. We talk to it, cherish it, nurture it, play with it and protect it. We circumcise it because we worry about its well-being. We have this exceptional relationship with our penis: an unbreakable bond that is developed through years of hard-core partnership. We love our penis because it gives us enormous pleasure and it stays with us through victories and defeats. No matter how fat or how old we get or how badly we behave, the penis always hangs around like a faithful buddy. Now, that's loyalty.

The circumcision master started muttering some Arabic words and grabbed the boy's equipment with a clamp. Then with an unexpected move, he cut off the skin. Blood spattered all over the place. The kid let out a loud scream that woke up the whole neighborhood.

I grabbed my crotch and turned around. The guy next to me fell on his knees and started barfing. The big guy across the room passed out. The lady next to him ran out of the room, screaming hysterically. The rest of the people in the room looked down with embarrassment. One drunken dude in the back started clapping and cheering like his favorite baseball team had just won the World Series. My son started laughing hysterically while pointing at the little kid.

I ran out of the house and jumped into my car. I sat behind the wheel, gasping for air. I could not believe what I had just witnessed. I pulled out my cell phone and called my mom. "Hey, Mom, remember my therapist said that I was traumatized at some point during my childhood? Was I circumcised in the hospital?"

"Well, son, your father and I don't like to talk about that incident. Let me put it this way: you were embarrassing, but the party was fabulous, and we beat the crap out of you that night."

My son came out of the house and got into the car, still laughing. "Dad, that was way too cool."

"That was sick," I said.

"Man, that's a cool job. How do you become a circumcision master? Do you think I should talk to my school counselor about this?"

"You are becoming a doctor, not a freakin' circumcision master."

"Hell no, Dad. I think I just found my true calling in life. I want to circumcise for a living."

"Are you crazy? Why would you wanna do that?"

"Dude, this is like the ultimate power. Like a freakin' ninja, I cut the guy's dong. That is just the coolest thing."

"You're not gay, are you?" I said.

"No, Dad, I'm not gay. I just think you get respect when you can chop off body parts like that."

"Kid, you really need to get off those stupid video games," I said.

"Dad, this has nothing to do with that. You should look at the big picture. I can rule. Like, I walk into a room and people step back 'cause I have the skills to do some serious damage."

I was convinced at that moment that my son was a few sandwiches short of a picnic. The kid had so much longing for power that he was willing to cut off other men's little heads to satisfy his ego. No doubt he was my son.

"Dad, are you circumcised?" my son asked.

"None of your business, why?"

"Just wanna know."

"Don't even think about it."

The kid was scaring me. I started to lock the door to my bedroom at night. I kept picturing him standing by my bed in the middle of the night with a razor and a clamp in his hands.

The kid got into trouble last year at school. The school's principal called me and said to go immediately to the school and meet him at his office. The principal was concerned. He told me that all the students in my son's class were asked to write an essay about their ideal profession and what they aspire to be when they grow up. The principal gave me my son's essay and asked me to read it.

Dear teacher,

I have given this subject a lot of thinking. I think I know what I want to be when I grow up. I want to be a torturer. My father is from Middle East and tells us stories about people in Middle East that get tortured all the time if they speak their mind. He tells us stories about people who want freedom but are sent to prisons and get tortured to forget about freedom. I think that's a cool job.

The guy who does the torturing can do anything that he wants. He can kick you or punch you or attach wires to your nipples and turn on the light. Then you'll be like electrocuted. I think that's cool.

But the torturer has to be careful not to electrocute himself while touching the wires. That would be bad and unprofessional.

I would like to know if there is a school that teaches you how to torture people. There must be a trade school with good classes so you can learn the latest in torture techniques. I torture my cat sometimes but he's too fast for me to chase.

My dad also tells us stories about people who get their hands and fingers cut off if they steal. He says that there are countries in the Middle East that punish their thieves by cutting off their body parts. I think that's cool.

If I failed the torture school and couldn't find a job in that profession, I would like to be the body part cutter. I think that would be a good job for me. I will start by cutting off small parts like the pinky and then as I learn the job I will cut bigger parts like legs and hands.

My friend, Joey, stole my favorite pen the other day and I wish I could cut off his hand. But when I'm officially employed by the body part cutting company, then I can do that.

I'm not sure if there are any schools for that. It should be like a medical school where they teach you how to use knifes to cut people up. I hope I can get accepted. I don't know how you practice to get good at cutting off body parts. I should practice on my cat or maybe Joey.

If I'm not successful in working in my favorite fields, I'll be very sad. I'm not sure how much money I'll be making if I become a torturer or a body part cutter but money is not that important. I think it's important to be happy about your job.

My dad wants me to be a doctor so I won't be a loser like him. He says that even though some doctors are nothing but a bunch of idiots but they make good money.

I don't want to be a doctor because I think it's boring. I heard from my friend Tommy that doctors stick their fingers in people's butt. I think that's gross.

I couldn't believe that my son wrote this essay. I was so proud of him. There were actually two sentences in that essay that had few or no grammatical errors. We had a writer in our family. That brought tears to my eyes.

The principal, on the other hand, was troubled. He suggested that my son should see the school psychologist. He thought that maybe my son was reaching out for help. I failed to see the problem here. I argued that the kid was just being a kid. But the principal was persistent, and he even went so far as to suggest that I, too, should see a psychologist.

I needed to have a man-to-man talk with the boy. Perhaps the principal was correct. Wanting to be a torturer was okay, but wanting to be a body part cutter was a bit odd. So I asked my son to come over to the kitchen for a talk. I needed to show maturity approaching this issue. What if the kid was really reaching out for help? What if the kid had real issues?

"What the hell was that essay all about? Are you crazy?"

"Dad, I wanna go to the Middle East with you. I wanna get a job there."

"Get a job doing what? Cutting people up?" I said.

"Yeah, there's a real need for that sort of job."

"I'm going to take you to the Middle East and commit you to a mental hospital. That's what I'm gonna do," I said.

"Come on, Dad. I really feel I can contribute. I have talents."

"You wouldn't last a day in the Middle East."

"Yes, I would."

"No, you wouldn't."

"Yes, I would."

"No, you wouldn't."

"Yes, I would."

Well, that went pretty well. I felt that the kid and I connected nicely. But the principal did not share my enthusiasm and held me legally accountable to take the kid to see a psychologist.

For many people, seeking help from a psychologist for mental issues is like seeing a specialist for eye or ear problems. Some people are open about their social anxieties and many speak openly about their sexual dysfunctions.

A Middle Easterner, however, never, ever, ever tells other Middle Easterners that he or she is seeing a psychologist. Because your character is judged by what you're hiding in your medicine cabinet. And you will automatically be labeled as schizophrenic, psychopathic, lunatic or even retarded. So you can imagine why I was hesitant to take my boy to see a shrink. But since I could have ended up in jail for not complying with principal's order, I took the necessary steps to introduce the boy to the world of mind therapy. After all, I was directly responsible for turning this kid into a fruitcake.

I made an appointment with the school-recommended psychologist and took the kid for consultation. The psychologist supposedly specialized in issues related to children of immigrants. She also had received some sort of an award for research she had done on immigrants' social and psychological issues.

The boy and I were sitting in the waiting room as the shrink walked out of her office and introduced herself. I liked what I saw. She was a very good-looking lady with long legs and beautiful eyes. What eye candy, I thought. If I had known how fine this little lady shrink was, I would've brought the whole family over a long time ago.

The lady psychologist read my son's file and asked me to stay in the room while she evaluated the boy. I was very happy to stay in the same room with her. The lady shrink explained that my son's behavior is not unusual for his age, and his wanting to pursue torture and mutilation as a career is not the worst thing she has heard of. She mentioned, however, that it's the school's responsibility to evaluate the kid's state of mind and detect any potential problem before it occurs.

I asked the lady shrink to take her time. We had all day.

"No, we don't," my son barked.

"Shut up when I'm talking to the lady," I said.

"I gotta study for a test," my son said.

"Study for a test? When did you learn those words?"

"Dad, you just wanna waste time here because you wanna boink her."

"What did you say?" I asked.

"You wanna get into her panties; that's why you're all smiling and shit."

Oh, the damn kid is too observant. Am I that obvious? I wanted to kill him for saying that.

"Why don't you two just calm down. Nobody is getting into anybody's panties. Not a chance," the lady shrink said, staring at me.

"What the hell am I here for?" my son asked.

"You are here because obviously there are certain things that bother you. Why don't you start by telling me what's bothering you?" the shrink said.

"Nothing."

"Do you like torturing people?"

"Depends."

"On what?"

"There are some people I like to torture," my son replied, looking at me.

"Like your dad?"

"Yeah, that would be a start."

I was ready to jump off the chair and choke the bastard. You want to torture me? You want a piece of me? Huh? I'm here. Come and get it.

"Why are you so mad at your father?" the lady shrink asked.

"Because."

"Because of?"

"Because he is stupid and only thinks with his little head instead of his big head."

"Excuse me?" I snapped.

"Sir, please keep quiet while your son expresses his feelings," the lady shrink said.

"I don't think with my little head," I said.

"Yes, you do. You're supposed to be the grownup. You never use your big head, only the little head. That's why Mom left us."

"And what do you mean by 'little head'?" the shrink asked.

"You know what I mean. Like he is sitting here right now looking at you and thinking with his little head."

The kid was beginning to frighten me. He knew me too well. For someone at that age, the kid had phenomenal intuition. I must have done something right.

Okay, the kid was right. I admit that the big head and the little head don't get along. There are tensions, conflicts and hostility. While the big head is busy making money and planning for the future, the little head blows all the money and doesn't give a hoot about the future. The big head desires bright women with good family upbringing and positive cash flow. The little head chases trashy bimbos with tattoos and IQs lower than nail polish.

The big head is focused on family and career; the little head is focused on peanuts and beer. The big head wants to change the world; the little head wants to do the world. The big head thinks; the little head drinks. The big head wants to commit; the little head wants to split. The big head cares about balances and checks; the little head cares about nothing but sex. The big head wants a woman with a beautiful heart; the little head wants any woman with her legs spread apart. The big head wants to learn a new trade; the little head only wants to get laid. The big head wants to get ahead; the little head wants to get a head.

Even though the big head occupies more space on the top, the little head wears the pants in the house. Eventually the big head understood the mighty power of the little head and gave up altogether. The big head is smart enough to know it's no match for a fun-loving, skirt-chasing, hard-drinking, badass like the little head. The little head is the king and that's that.

Like many hot-blooded Iranian men, I have been held hostage by my own little head. The little head is doing the thinking and the big head, not happy with the situation, has packed its bags and moved out. The little head is the decision maker. So I do what the little head tells me. My son was right on.

The lady shrink looked at me with resentment the way my ex-wife used to do. I'm thinking, wait up, we just met, give it a day or two before hating me. The lady shrink turned her attention back to my son. "Do you think your father makes you want to torture people?"

"Yeah."

"Why is that?"

"He is like this FOB dude from, like, another planet. He doesn't let me do my thing. He's constantly in my face, 'do this, do that.' I'm like, man, chill already."

"Wait a minute," I said. "What the hell did you just say?"

The lady shrink looked at me like I was an idiot. She turned her chair and faced me. "Your son is suffocating. That's what he is saying."

"Suffocating?"

"Yes he needs space, privacy and bit of a creative freedom. I see this all the time in immigrant families; the kids feel they're suffocating because their parents block their sense of freedom and creativity. The kids don't feel they belong because they're restricted by their parents' cultural hang-ups."

"Are you sure?"

"Am I sure? Excuse me? I do this for a living, you know."

This was the biggest bull I'd ever heard. I couldn't take this anymore. I looked deeply into the lady shrink's eyes and said, "Can I ask you a personal question?"

The lady shrink was a bit surprised, but she managed to keep her professional composure. "A personal question?"

"Yes, can I ask you a personal question?"

"Sure."

"Do you have kids?"

"No, but I'm a trained professional."

"I understand that you are a trained professional but have you ever raised a kid? I'm talking changing diapers, wiping shit off their ass, teaching them to walk, talk, ride a bike and all that crap."

"No."

"Well, then listen up. Kids are smarter than you and I. They learn to manipulate to get their way, they can smell weakness. My son here has been craving the Alien Sky video game for the past three months. I told him that he is not getting it because the game is violent, pointless and a waste of time. Knowing that when I say NO that means NO, the kid came up with an alternative plan to get his way—that's what kids do."

"I'm not following," she said.

"Well, let me explain," I said. "He is smart enough to know that the school system in this country is a reactionary entity that avoids liability at all costs. So he writes an essay that would raise a red flag and create panic. A son of a Middle Eastern immigrant who wants to become a torturer, now that will get some attention, wouldn't you think?"

"I guess," she said.

"So the kid knows that this essay is his ticket to having the video game because his dad will be called in, and then he will be sent to see a therapist, and the therapist will recommend that the dad should be a little easy on the kid. And, of course, the dad, who is Middle Eastern and doesn't want trouble with the school system and authorities, will get scared and do what the kid wants."

The lady shrink cleared her throat and looked at my son. She then turned her attention back to me and asked, "But how do you know all that?"

"Because I would've done the same thing myself. I raised this kid. I taught him everything he knows. I can read him like an old book. That's called parenthood, which is a pure learning experience, and it's all about instincts, and there are no degrees and no professional training out there that can teach you that."

The psychologist looked at my son and asked, "Is that true?"

"Yeah. All the kids at school have that game except me."

"And you wrote that essay to get your father in trouble?"

"Yeah. All the kids at school have that game except me."

"Do you understand what you have done?"

"Yeah. All the kids at school have that game except me."

"Okay, you said that already."

"Yeah. All the kids at school have that game except me."

"Shut up," the shrink said.

"Hey, I'm a kid; you can't tell me to shut up," my son said.

"Yes, I can."

"No, you can't."

"Yes, I can."

"No, you can't."

This had gone far enough. I had to stop it. "Hey, both of you shut up. Am I the only adult in this room?"

The room went quiet. There was an awkward silence. My son wasn't expecting to be outnumbered in this place, and he certainly didn't expect to be yelled at by the psychologist. And I could clearly see that the shrink was unhappy about being yelled at by the father of a patient. It was very complex.

I found two people in front me whose egos needed a little massaging. One was my son, whose brilliant plan didn't quite work out, and the other, of course, was the little psychologist babe who was served by a chauvinistic Middle Eastern hooligan. I wanted this moment to last forever. For once I was respected by my adversaries. This was a precious moment. Where is a camera when you need one?

The shrink was smart enough to realize that my boy was just another teenaged con artist who had subscribed to the idea that if you can't have it the honest way, try cheating. She wrote a letter to the principal and declared my son a non-threatening subject who needed a lot more homework and after-school activities.

Now, it was my turn to go to work. I asked the lady psychologist out on a date, but she declined and said that she was a lesbian.

"Are you sure?" I asked.

"Am I sure that I'm a lesbian, or am I sure that I don't wanna go out with you?" she answered.

"Are you sure you're a lesbian?"

"Last time I checked."

"So you tellin' me that guys do nothing for you?" I said.

"Not a thing."

"Like, if Brad Pitt was standing here naked, you wouldn't feel a thing."

"No."

"Nothing at all, not even a little twitch?"

"None."

"Give me a chance; maybe I can convert you back," I said.

"Men like you are the reason I became lesbian in the first place."

Even I, with all my limited social know-how, understand that there is something seriously wrong when a woman labels herself lesbian to avoid going out with me. But I was not going to take no for answer. So I kept calling her day and night, and I disturbed her so much that she finally gave in and said yes. I looked at this as an opportunity to bring a woman from lesbianism back to heterosexualism.

So she and I were having dinner at this expensive restaurant. She hadn't slapped me or run out screaming, so I assumed she was having a good time. The waiter started taking our order. She ordered the most expensive items on the menu. She just went on and on. Quite an appetite for a little woman, I thought. I made a quick calculation and realized, so far, she had cost me over $300. The woman would not stop ordering.

After the waiter left, she gave me the nastiest look and said, "You have been making my life a living hell, so I'm gonna give you a lesson you'll not forget. I am going to order everything on the menu and make you pay for it, you son of a bitch. This will be a lesson for you not to harass women and to understand the meaning of the word NO. I am going to make you spend so much money, you'll be on welfare for the next six months."

"You're kidding, right?"

"Do I look like I'm kidding? Huh? Do I?" she said

It was a setup. This woman was going to make me pay for all my sins. My date's agenda was to make me regret all those times I treated women like sexual objects. This was a nightmare; it cannot be happening to me. I was not only embarrassed, I felt stupid.

Just when I thought things couldn't get worse, my cousin Reza, *El Cheapo*, walked into the restaurant. What the hell was he doing here? This is not the kind of place he would ever go for dinner. I tried avoiding eye contact at all cost, but it was too late. Reza spotted me and made his way to our table.

"Hey, coz, long time."

"Yeah, I'm busy," I said.

"Thanks for delivering my cake."

"Forget about it, okay. It's not a good time," I said.

"Who is the chick?"

"This is my date. She is a psychologist."

Reza said hello to the shrink lady. He looked curiously worried. He kept scanning the place like he was hiding from someone.

"Can I talk to you in private?" Reza asked.

"No, I'm on a date."

"Please, it's a matter of life and death," Reza said.

I excused myself and walked to the bar with him.

"Listen, I'm sorry about the damn cake. I'll pay you back," I said.

"It's not about the cake; I need to borrow your date."

"Excuse me?"

"I'm meeting these Arab investors here," Reza said. "These guys are old school, real estate investment, we're talking millions. This is the opportunity of a lifetime. I'm supposed to meet them here with the wife. They're big on family and shit like that. If I don't have the wife with me, they won't give me a dime; they don't deal with single guys."

"So bring your damn wife."

"Had a big fight. She left me."

"When did that happen?" I asked.

"Last month."

"This is ridiculous," I said. "My date will never go for it. She is a respectable lesbian. You've got to be out of your mind to even consider this. This is an insult. How would you feel if I asked you to lend me your wife?"

Reza looked around and said, "How much?"

"Pardon?"

"How much for your date?"

"Are you for real?" I said.

"Would a thousand dollars do?"

That's it. Now I was really pissed. I was going to kick his ass. How dare he offer me money for my date? Who the hell does he think he is? This rich boy thinks he can just walk in and buy his way through everything in life.

On the other hand, a thousand dollars could pay for a nice set of new tires for my car with enough money left over to fix that radiator leak, but I was not going to sink that low. I was not going to step on my dignity and honor for thousand dollars. I was not going to make a bigger fool of myself in front of my date. I'm not that cheap.

I looked at Reza with disgust and said, "Two thousand and she's yours."

"Done," Reza said while pulling hundred dollar bills out of his pocket. He gave me twenty brand-new Ben Franklins and said, "Why don't you take a hike. I'll talk to the girl. I think she likes me."

"She's crazy about hairy guys," I said.

"Oh, yeah?" Reza said.

"Yeah, she said it herself."

"This is gonna be easier than I thought," Reza said.

"Go get her, big boy."

Reza unbuttoned his shirt all the way down to his bellybutton, exposing the massive black jungle residing on his chest. Reza was so hairy, one day when he was visiting the zoo, a monkey made a pass at him. He was so hairy that when he went to a drugstore to buy sunscreen, the counter boy fell on the ground, laughing. Reza was selected as the number-one donor to the Hair Club for Men five years running.

Reza walked to her table and sat down. I looked at my date from a distance. The table was full of plates, and she was still ordering more food. I made a quick run to the exit. I grabbed the waiter on the way out and told him, "You see that gentleman sitting at my table? He'll pick up the check."

I learned my lesson that night: treat women with respect and bring your checkbook if you're on a date with a pissed-off lesbian.

Back to my son. Don't get me wrong, I have some good times with my son, too. I think the best experience I had with him was when he asked me to teach him the principles of kissing men! That's right, kissing men is something we Middle Easterners do. It has no sexual significance and it is purely social. It's a form of greeting, love and affection in a most primitive way. I'm sure you have seen Middle Eastern men kiss each other on the cheeks. I admit that it's a bit odd, but it's mostly ceremonial.

This is how it goes: you walk into a room full of people, start kissing the closest guy standing next to you, and make your way around the room. It might take ten minutes to finish the kissing fest. And then if you step out of the room for, let's say, twenty minutes to smoke and catch your breath, upon your return to the room you have to start kissing everybody again.

"Hey, get over here and give me a kiss; long time no see."

"What do you mean 'long time no see'? I kissed your ugly face twenty minutes ago."

My son needed to learn the art of kissing men since he was old enough to be treated like any other male member of the family. Since I had friends and family coming over to our house on a regular basis, my son was grabbed and kissed by other male members of the family. The poor kid hated this gesture and mostly stayed in his room and away from our guests. But he had no choice except to come out of his room every once in a while to use the bathroom or to eat, and as soon as he walked out of his room, WHAM, he was grabbed and kissed by all the male guests.

The poor kid realized that kissing men comes with the territory, and no matter what he did, he could not avoid it. After all he was a byproduct of a failed Iranican marriage, and unless he moved out of the state, he had to occasionally kiss men. So he came to me for advice. The kid had so many questions, like how to avoid the lips? How to initiate minimal contact? How to dodge the mighty Iranian nose? Did he kiss twice or three times? And by the way, what was the difference between kissing twice and three times anyway? How to avoid rashes and zits? Does he wipe his face, or does he allow the spit to sit there for a while? There was so much to learn in such a short time.

I, myself, am not very big on kissing men. Living in America, you develop social skills which do not include physical contact with males other than a simple handshake or a high five. Though the majority of my social interactions revolve around my Iranian friends, we simply do not kiss each other. I know it's a form of greeting, brotherhood, tradition, affection or whatnot. But the sheer idea of kissing another man is extremely revolting to me.

I perhaps developed this phobia from my father. He is a very loving individual and, like any hot-blooded Iranian man, he likes to show affection by slapping big slobbery kisses on the cheeks. However, the problem is his incredibly huge and bushy mustache. He has a mustache made for kings of the early Persian Empire. It starts from his big nose and moves down to the sides of his face and immaculately points up to the sky on both sides.

When I kiss my father, I have to close my eyes for fear of getting poked in the eye by his mustache, which can cause permanent damage. I also fear that his mustache might end up in my nose—not to mention the three-day skin rash caused by thick and unforgiving facial hair. A traditional friend of mine claims that kissing guys is a sign of manhood. Well, I simply fail to find manhood in kissing men. But my son, like me, needed to accept the tradition and go with it.

He needed a teacher. He was the grasshopper in need of a master. He was Luke Skywalker and needed Yoda's help. He was the Karate Kid desperate for Mister Miyagi. He was the Buddhist monk in search of the Dalai Lama. Well, you get the point.

But I was in no form or shape an authority on the art of kissing men. And I certainly was not qualified to teach my son lessons in the art. At a moment of panic, desperation and exhaustion, I found the answer. It was in front of me all along, but I was cursed with such monumental ignorance that I almost missed it altogether.

"Hey, Dad, do you have a moment?" I asked my father.

"What is it? I am busy watching this stupid Iranian satellite program. The damn thing shows five minutes of programs and twenty minutes of commercials. How many Iranian realtors can we have in this town?"

"Dad, the time has come for you and your grandson to have a man-to-man talk. He has questions and he desperately needs some answers."

"You want me to talk to him about using condoms?"

"No, I'll do that myself. What I mean is this kissing business, you know, kissing guys."

"Why? Is he gay?"

"No, I'm talking about kissing guys on the cheek as a form of greeting, like, when you go to parties and you have to kiss all the guys on the cheeks as you walk in."

"Oh, I see where you're going with that," Dad said. "Bring the kid over and let me teach him what I know."

I took my son over to my father's house. My father came downstairs and sat in front of my son.

"Well, lad, I'll tell you what I know, and then it's all up to you to apply the art."

This was great. My son was benefiting from seventy years of pure Iranian kissing experience. He was being taught by the best of the best, a man who has mastered all the moves, techniques and formations. The one who can teach my son the tricks of the trade. The one who has not lost any of his traditional Iranian foundation and is willing to lead a young man through the great odyssey of life.

"Well, son, make no mistake about it," my father said. "Kissing a man's face is more than a simple act of affection. It's the manifestation of power and social importance. It's the public projection of a powerful social and economic position. A position that should be presented as fundamentally strong and unshakable."

My boy stared at his grandfather like he was attending the Communist party's propaganda meeting.

"Dad, what did he just say?" my son asked me.

"Be quiet and listen to the man," I replied.

"What I'm trying to say, son," my father continued, "is that by kissing properly and powerfully, you show the other guy that you are in control of the situation and you are a power to be reckoned with."

There was much more to this than I originally thought.

"You guys are gay," my son said.

"Shut up and listen," my dad snapped at the kid. "First you look deep in the other guy's eyes. A look that projects power yet respect. Then you move close to him with your right hand extended in a forty-degree angle. You shake hands with a powerful grip. A kind of a grip that says HEY, MAN, I DON'T TAKE CRAP FROM NO ONE. The stronger his grip, the harder you squeeze."

My kid practiced his handshake with me.

"Now comes the moment where you need to position your body. Balance is the key. You will not move toward the guy, as this will signal weakness. You will pull the guy forward with a swift hip rotation using your torso while throwing your weight in the opposite direction."

This was getting too complicated. The kid started taking notes.

"Now, you have to be careful since the other guy might be a pro, and he might counterattack your move with a reverse shoulder fake. This will throw you off balance and will force you to move toward him. You can counter his strategy by utilizing his momentum and catching him off guard with a swift shoulder alignment."

The kid practiced his shoulder rotation.

"Now comes the hard part. This is when you need to force the issue. You will be the one who determines which cheek will be kissed first. If the guy is uncoordinated or unable to make up his mind, you need to take it upon yourself to direct his head towards your right shoulder with a soft but effective head butt. This is critical since the direction of the kiss will be determined at this moment. You will assess the situation with watchful eyes and avoid lips at any cost. If the guy's lips, for any reason, are in your way, immediately perform the second head butt with authority."

"Man, you guys are gross," my son said. I told him to pay attention. There would be a written exam after this.

"Once cheek contact is established," my father continued, "turn your head slightly to the right and dismount with a quick and unexpected move. Tilt your head back as far as you possibly can to avoid contact with obstacles such as glasses, big nose or both. You are almost done. Now you need to complete the second part. You should take advantage of the momentum and move your head to the left. You will apply the same movements and principles to the other side of the face with powerful and authoritarian moves. Once the kiss has been completed, you will put your left hand on the person's shoulder and dismount."

Whoa! This man really knows his kiss. I was impressed by my father's knowledge on the subject. He opened my son's eyes to a world he never knew existed. He showed my son the knowledge possessed only by masters. The man is my hero. I never knew kissing another man carried so much politics. I never imagined that a simple act of welcoming could signal so many social implications. I understood the delicate balance of power and prestige. It all made sense now. My son, on the other hand, ran to the bathroom and gagged.

But I was sure that my son was ready to face the best of them. He knew what to do and how to control the situation now. I watched him apply his newly acquired skills, and he was like the puppet master. I was so proud. He could move in and out, side to side, up and down. He was like a pro basketball player. Fake left, move right.

I could see my son developing his own system now. He would move in, kiss twice and move out like a woodpecker. They didn't even know what hit them. He was sensational. He developed a technique custom made to his height, weight and style. It brought tears to my eyes.

10. You Want To Date My Daughter? I Don't Think So

I'M TRADITIONAL WHEN IT COMES TO MY DAUGHTER dating at a young age. I can't help it. I know it's wrong, but I just can't see my teenaged girl alone with a stranger. It kills me. I think the main reason I don't let my daughter date is because I know my kind. I'm a guy and I was a teen once. I know what goes on in their minds and it scares me.

Teenaged boys don't care about relationships. They're not in it to meet and marry a nice girl. They are not planning their future or trying to find that special someone. They are not out there to overcome loneliness or find their soul mates.

Teenaged boys have testosterone oozing out of their pimples, and the only thing they have in mind is to get their hands on the goods—and that, my friends, I'll not allow. They can get their hands on the goods—but not my goods.

Like many Middle Eastern-American men, I want my daughter to live at home until she is married. I certainly don't want her to date—at least not until she is well into her thirties. I don't like my daughter to smoke, drink, use makeup or watch too much television. The rules are simple: all she needs to do is to concentrate on her schoolwork and hang out with her girlfriends. That's all.

The thing that scares me the most is the possibility of my daughter getting herself mixed up with drugs. Don't get me wrong, I have nothing against drug users. As a matter of fact, I think drug users are fantastic people. Let me reiterate: I believe drug users are the backbone of every strong society.

Now, spare me the victim talk. I have no tolerance for heart-breaking sociopolitical analysis of this so-called crisis. I have no interest in sentiments on how sick human society has become because of illegal drugs. I don't think so. I think drug use is good for any nation. I think nations are benefiting greatly from illegal drugs.

I don't think of drug users as victims because they make a choice. They puff the magic flute simply because they enjoy it, not because there is a gun pointing at their heads. Maybe they do it because they want to escape harsh realities of life, or maybe they do it to get a good high and hallucinate for a while. Every man has a right to hallucinate, don't you think?

Lack of ambition is what makes drug users good citizens. That's right folks, junkies are good for society because, unlike other assholes, they have no desire to change the world, lead revolutions, run for president, start socialist workers parties, kill or torture opponents, preach religion, go to war for oil, steal stock holders' money, run for senate or congress, commit terrorist acts, blow up innocent people, or assassinate journalists. Sharon, Milosevic, Saddam, and Osama aren't drug users. Neither were Mussolini, Hitler, Ayatollah, or Stalin.

Drug users are completely harmless because they hardly ever leave home. They are busy getting high all the time. When they are not high, they are too lazy to even go to the bathroom to relieve themselves. That's my kind of a guy. That's why every society needs good old-fashioned, lazy junkies who have no energy to butt into other people's business. But the rules certainly don't apply for my daughter.

Of course, what I think does not carry much weight around my household. I'm invisible. When I talk to my daughter, I feel like I'm talking to a wall. The Persian Barbie has her own agenda. I guess my strict rules have pushed her underground. She does things behind my back and lies to me all the time. I know she smokes, and I can tell she uses makeup as soon as she leaves the house. The girl is boy-crazy and she's not shy about it either.

She came to me once and asked if she could go on a double date with her friend. The answer was no.

"Why not?"

"Because you're too young."

"I'm fifteen."

"Hang in there for another fifteen years, and you'll be on your way."

"Another fifteen years? I'll be an old maid."

"There are plenty of guys out there who would love to go out with an old maid," I said.

"Nobody dates old maids."

"Not true," I said. "Guys love old maids. There is a video out there called, 'Old Maids Gone Wild.' They can't keep them on the shelf."

"Dad, all my friends are dating except me."

"If all your friends jumped off a building, would you do that, too?"

"Yeah, hello," she said.

"Kid, we really need to talk."

"Dad, please let me go on this date. The guy is a dream.

All the girls at school are in love with him."

"My answer is final. You are dating nobody until you're ready."

"Dad, I'm ready."

"You'll be ready when I say you are. Now go to your room and hit the books or do whatever you do in there."

My daughter stormed into her room and slammed the door shut. Since I can read my kids' minds, I knew she would immediately get on the phone and call her best friend. So I did what every sensible parent in my shoes would do: I picked up the phone and listened to her conversation.

"I hate him; I just hate my dad," my daughter told her friend while crying.

"Your dad is stupid. Why is he, like, so strict?" her friend asked.

"I wish I could have him deported. Like illegal aliens."

"Why don't you? He is so, like, stupid."

"I really wanna see Billy. He is so dreamy."

"He is totally cool and he is, like, so cute. You're so lucky he wants to go out with you."

"What should I do?" my daughter asked.

"Like, tell your dad you're staying at my house, and then, like, we go meet the guys; it would be, like, so much fun."

"You think that would work?"

"Sure, I'll get my older sister to call your dad and pretend, like, she's my mom. Then she'll tell your dad you're gonna spend the night. It'll totally work."

"You would do that?" my daughter asked.

"Sure. What are friends for?"

"Oh, I can't wait to see Billy."

"Yeah, me, too… I mean, yeah, that would be cool."

I was furious at my daughter. I wanted to barge into her room and take her head off. She was plotting against me at the tender age of fifteen. Imagine what she will do to me when she is in her twenties.

I had two alternatives: one was to confront her and give her a piece of my mind (not that I had any to spare), or I could play along, let things unfold and catch her red-handed. Yeah, the second option would work better. She will learn a lesson in front of her friends and I'll be entertained.

I received the phone call the next day. The older sister puts on a good show, introduces herself as the mother of my daughter's best friend, and informs me of a slumber party at her house, which, of course, my daughter was invited to attend.

"Absolutely, it'll be my pleasure to drop her off," I said.

"No, that's okay. I'll send my oldest daughter to come and pick her up."

"Well, that's wonderful. Thank you so much for inviting my daughter."

"No, thank you."

"No, really, thank you."

A few hours later, my daughter came downstairs all dressed up and ready to go.

"Awfully dressed up for a slumber party," I said.

"Dad, this is how girls dress for slumber parties; you don't know anything."

"I see. I guess you're right. I don't know anything."

The doorbell rang and my daughter zoomed out of the house. She ran toward a small car parked outside and got in. The car took off like a bat out of hell. I immediately ran outside, got into my car and followed the small car. This was like a cop movie. I was keeping my distance and tailing the car like I was a detective chasing America's most wanted criminals. Years of watching stupid cop movies were paying off.

The small car pulled into a mall's parking lot and stopped in front of the main entrance. My daughter and her best friend got out. A few words were exchanged between my daughter's best friend and the driver, the small car took off, and my daughter and her best friend walked into the mall.

I found a place to park my car and ran inside. I had to stay out of sight and watch the situation develop. My daughter and her best friend walked up to the food court and met up with two high school boys. One of the boys, presumably Billy, kissed my daughter on the cheek. I was about to explode. This Billy boy was going to pay for this.

Billy looked like a super deluxe punk straight out of a rock concert. He looked as if he had not combed his hair in the last ten years, his arms were covered with tattoos and his face was pierced with rings and ornaments. Billy's jeans had two holes in the back, which exposed his butt cheeks like two shiny head lights. This was the devil himself, and my daughter's choice in men was disappointing from the get-go.

I needed a plan. I grabbed my cell phone and called my buddy Ali *The Nose*. Ali is a wicked looking man with the biggest nose. He was perfect for my plan.

"Ali, grab two knives and two scarves and meet me at the mall." I said.

"What the heck is going on?" Ali asked.

"Just get your ass here. Don't forget the stuff I asked for."

"Are you okay?"

"No, I'm not okay. Just get over here, now."

I hung up the phone and watched my daughter and Billy from a distance. Billy was sucking on his soda pop and rubbing my daughter's hand. He was putting the moves on my girl. I was seeing red. I started breathing hard. I thought I was having a heart attack. I couldn't take this any more. Luckily, Ali lived only a few blocks from the mall.

Fifteen minutes later, I saw Ali wandering inside the mall, looking for me. I grabbed his shoulder and pulled him into a store.

"What the hell is the matter with you?" Ali asked.

"Did you bring the stuff?"

"Yeah, it's in my pocket. What's going on?"

"My daughter is on a date with a high school guy. She lied to me. The guy is putting on the moves. I want to scare the guy off and I need your help."

"That's all?" Ali asked.

"What do you mean? This is important to me, can't you see?"

"Okay, I'm at your service. Tell me what you want me to do," Ali said.

"Okay, listen. The kid has been drinking his soda like a fish. Sooner or later he is going to use the restroom. You'll go into the restroom, get inside a stall, cover your face with one of the scarves and hold on to the knife. I'll follow the kid inside the restroom and push him inside the stall. Together, we'll threaten to kill him if he touches my daughter."

Ali looked at me like I was crazy. "Don't you think that's a bit extreme?"

"I'm just gonna scare him, you bonehead. Nobody is going to kill anybody."

"I understand that, but still the word 'kill' is such an ugly word. Maybe you should say you will harm him instead of kill him," Ali said, looking down at the floor.

"Harm, kill, what's the difference?"

"Well, we certainly don't want to scar the kid for life," Ali said.

"Is that your daughter out there getting her hands rubbed by a high school boy? Is that your daughter out there getting…"

"Okay, okay, I get your point, but I still think threatening to kill the kid is a bit too much."

"Get your ass inside the restroom, and give me my scarf and knife."

"Okay, I'll see you in the restroom," Ali said as he reluctantly walked away.

I went back to my strategic location and waited. The kid was getting more aggressive by the minute, and my daughter was not putting up much of a fight either. I wanted to kill both of them now. Oh, the rage.

Billy excused himself and walked to the bathroom. I was right behind him as we both got inside and walked to a standup urinal. There were two other people in the bathroom. I stood next to Billy, waiting for the opportunity to strangle him. I was thinking of fifty different ways I wanted to skin him alive. The other two individuals left the bathroom, and it was me and Billy. The time had arrived.

I walked behind Billy, put on my scarf, covered his mouth, grabbed him and pulled him inside a stall. The stall was empty.

"Ali, were the hell are you?" I yelled.

"I'm here," Ali's voice came from the stall next door.

"Get over here," I said.

"I'm busy."

"Busy doing what?"

"I'm taking care of the business," Ali said.

"Business?"

"Yeah, I had to go."

"Couldn't you find a better time?"

"Sorry, I couldn't help it."

"Number one or number two?" I asked.

"Well, it's the damn shish kabob I had last night. It's a big number two. Sorry."

"Goddamn it, Ali. Get your ass over here."

"I can't. I gotta wipe."

"Hurry up and wipe, damn it, wipe."

"Okay, don't rush me," Ali said.

I uncovered Billy's mouth. The kid gasped for air. I pulled out the knife and held it to his throat. I saw the knife for the first time. It was a small butter knife. Billy and I stared at the knife. It certainly wasn't as intimidating as I had hoped.

"I got no money, man," Billy said.

"I don't want your money," I whispered.

"Are you, like, a terrorist?"

"Oh, you have no idea," I replied with my best terrorist accent.

Meanwhile, next door, Ali was making hurtful noises that would make a grown man bawl.

"Ali, is the alien out yet?" I yelled.

"Almost there. Don't rush me."

I got in Billy's face. "What's your name?"

"Billy."

"How old are you?"

"Seventeen."

"Who is that girl you are with?"

"I don't know. Some freshman chick at school."

"What are you planning to do with her?"

"I don't know, like, kiss and stuff."

"Kiss?"

"Maybe. I don't know," Billy said.

"Do you know who she is?"

"Yeah, she's some chick at school."

"I'll tell you who she is," I said. "She is the daughter of Saddam Hussein. I'm Saddam's bodyguard, and if anybody touches Saddam's daughter, I have no choice but to kill him in a flash."

Billy swallowed hard. "No way, dude."

"Way."

"Dude, I had, like, no idea. Are you gonna kill me?"

"I have to; if I don't kill you, Saddam is gonna kill me."

"I'll scream," Billy said.

"I'll cut you up before the sound leaves your mouth. I'm a trained killer."

"You're gonna kill me with a butter knife?" Billy said.

"Yes. Your death shall be painful and calculated," I replied with a grin.

Wide-eyed, Billy pissed in his pants.

"Did you just piss in your pants?" I asked, jumping out of the way.

"Hell yeah, dude. I saw this movie once, like, the dude killed his roommate with a butter knife. It was gruesome."

Ali finally decided to join us. He was a mess. His shoes were untied and his fly was open. Poor Billy was having a heart attack now.

I looked at Ali and nodded in the direction of his pants.

"What?" Ali said.

"Your fly is open," I whispered.

"Oh, sorry. I always do that."

Billy looked at Ali and smiled. "Dude, do you, like, take your shoes off when you shit?"

Ali looked down at his shoes. "Yes I do. Makes me feel more relaxed."

"Dude, I do the exact same thing. I can't shit with my shoes on."

Ali and Billy gave each other a high five. I couldn't believe my eyes.

"Hey," I snapped at Billy. "You got more important things to worry about."

Ali looked at Billy's soaking-wet pants. "Did the kid piss in his pants?"

"Yeah, I did man," Billy said. "This dude scared the shit out of me."

Disgruntled, Ali took off his scarf and yelled at me. "See what you did? The kid pissed in his pants; are you happy now?"

"Put on your scarf, you idiot."

"No, I will not put on my scarf until you tell the kid he will not die."

"Yes, he will," I said. "I can not disobey Saddam's direct order."

"Who?" Ali asked.

"Saddam. Remember we work for Saddam, and we are here to protect his daughter."

"We are?" Ali said.

"Yes, we are."

"Oh, yeah, Saddam. That's right. We do work for the man," Ali said.

Billy looked at us suspiciously and said, "Wait a minute. Didn't they, like, catch Saddam awhile back?"

Ali and I looked at each other, surprised. The kid kept up with the news and current affairs!

"That was one of his doubles. Nobody can catch Saddam," I replied.

"That's right. Saddam is in Hawaii," Ali said.

I lowered my knife and faced Ali. "So what do you think we should do? Should we kill him or let him go?"

"Let me go. Please let me go," Billy said. "I'll never talk to her again. I swear, I'll never even look at her again."

Ali ran a trembling hand through his hair. "Well, the kid seems sincere. Maybe we should trust him."

"I don't know," I replied. "Saddam is going to be awfully mad if he finds out we let him go easy. Maybe we should cut off his fingers."

"No, dude. I wanna be a rock star, man. I need the fingers to play the guitar."

"Maybe we should cut off his testicles instead. You know Saddam needs new testicles for his collection," I said.

"Testicles?" Billy cried out. "Dude, cut off the fingers but not the testicles, please."

"I'll talk to Saddam myself," Ali replied. "Maybe I can change his mind; after all, he is my father."

"No way, dude. Saddam is your dad? That's far out," Billy said.

Ali had given the story a whole new twist. I liked it.

"In that case, we'll let him go, but only under one condition," I said.

"What? I'll do anything, dude." Billy said.

"You'll tell all the other guys at school that she is the daughter of Saddam, and if anybody asks her out on a date, he will die."

"Totally, dude. I'll get on with it tomorrow. I swear nobody will go near her."

Ali opened the door and kicked Billy out. Poor Billy ran for his life. Ali and I stood there in the stall reflecting on what we had just done. Was it the right thing to do? Absolutely not. Do I feel awful about what we just did to Billy? Yes, I do. Am I a retard? Yes, I am.

"Saddam's son, huh?" I asked Ali.

"Sure," Ali replied. "I had fantasies about being Saddam's son. Imaging doing anything you like and getting away with it. That, my friend, is the ultimate fantasy of every man. There is Saddam's son in every one of us. The difference is, they could get away with it and the rest of us can't."

"Well, the bastards are dead."

"Yeah, and that's what made the story so fascinating."

Ali and I left the restroom and walked back to our cars. I thanked Ali for his brilliant performance and asked him what he thought about what I did today. "You are a father; you have your faults but your heart is in the right place."

I'm not sure if that was a compliment or an insult. I went home and thought about what I did. It just didn't feel right. I could not chase my daughter around twenty-four hours a day and constantly threaten to kill every guy that talked to her. There must be another way. The more I kept her from dating, the bigger the idea got in her head.

My daughter's popularity took a nosedive as a result of my action. When she walked into the classroom, all the boys ran out. When she went into the cafeteria and sat at a table, the table cleared. She was eventually told by her friends that a rumor had been circulating in the school that linked her to Saddam's family.

"Dad, people at school think I'm Saddam's daughter."

"Really? Amazing how close-minded people can be. Just because your parents have a Middle Eastern background, they automatically assume you're related to Saddam or Osama. Kids can be so cruel," I replied while hiding my face.

"Dad, if I just knew who started the rumor, I could kill her."

"Easy, honey, before you know, it will be forgotten."

"But my life is a disaster. None of the boys talk to me."

"That's awful, honey. Anything I can do to help? I can come to school and talk to the boys."

"That's okay, Dad. I don't want you anywhere near my school. You'd probably make things worse."

Here we go again. My plans flopped. I'm a horrible father. My daughter was hurting and it was my fault. That did not make me happy. What did I do? A fifteen-year-old should not be stressing over meeting stupid guys. I had to do something. I could see the pain in my daughter's eyes and that was killing me. It's amazing how children constantly pay for their parents' stupidity.

I called Ali *The Nose* and explained that our plan had backfired.

"Our plan?" he asked. "That was your plan and I was just helping you out."

"Okay, I know, but I can't see my girl suffer like this. I need to undo what I did."

"How you gonna do that?"

"I have some ideas and I need your help."

"I'll be more than happy to help."

"Thanks, buddy. I owe you one," I said.

"No, you'll owe me more than one."

"Whatever."

"Okay, what is your plan?" Ali asked

I picked up Ali at his apartment, drove to my daughter's school and parked the car cross the street from the school. Ali and I were sitting patiently in the car waiting for the kids to start making their way out of the school and leave for the day. I looked at Ali and asked, "Did you bring the scarves and the knives?"

"I brought the scarves but there was a problem with knives."

"What sort of a problem?" I asked.

"Well, you know I don't wash dishes till I run out—right? So I didn't have any clean knives."

"So what did you bring?"

Ali pulled out two forks.

"You brought forks?" I asked.

"Sorry, that's all I had."

"Great. Why didn't you bring some spoons as backup?"

"Hey, take it or leave it," Ali said.

"Fine."

"Fine."

I pulled a fork out of his hand and put it in my side pocket.

School was out and the kids started to flock onto the street. I spotted Billy in the crowd. He said goodbye to his buddies and began walking down the street towards his house. I made a U-turn and followed him from behind. Billy kept on walking and eventually made his way to a side street.

Sensing that someone was following him, Billy looked back and spotted my car. Poor Billy began running like a deer being chased by a pack of lions in the sub-Saharan wilderness of Africa. I stepped on the gas pedal and caught up with him. Billy made a right turn and ran into a dead-end alley. His ass belonged to me.

I stopped the car at the entrance of the alley and stared at Billy, who was trapped. I revved the engine. Billy stared at me with the uncertainty of a cat trapped in a basement corner. Ali jumped out of the car, snatched Billy, threw him into the back seat, pulled out his fork and held it close to Billy's neck. Billy pissed his pants.

"Oh, man, you need to stop pissing in your pants," Ali said while backing away from Billy.

"Sorry, dudes. I can't help it. You guys scare the shit of me," Billy said.

"You are seventeen years old for God's sake; you should have some control over your bladder," Ali said.

"Dude, I lose it when I get nervous. Ever since I was a kid, I've had that problem."

"I'm sorry," Ali said while lowering his fork. "I can be scary sometimes."

There was a moment of uncertainty among the three of us. I had to change the subject to get Billy's mind off his little accident.

"Do you know why you're here?" I asked Billy.

"Dudes, I swear I did as you guys told me. I told all the guys at school to stay away from her. I swear I did it."

"I know," I replied, "and Saddam wanted to extend his gratitude for a job well done."

"No kidding. He said that himself?" Billy said.

"Yes, he did. As a matter of fact, you did so well, he has another mission for you."

"Far out, dude; like, what is it?" Billy asked.

"He wants you to go out with his daughter."

Billy panicked in the back seat. "Hell no, dudes, you guys think I'm stupid? I ain't going on no date with her again. You guys are setting me up. Like, I'm gonna fall for that old trick."

"Listen, you little shit, don't you get cute on me," I snapped. "You don't say no to Saddam. Saddam gets what Saddam wants, and he wants you to pick up his daughter at her house and take her on a date. Of course, there are conditions."

"Like what?"

"You will not touch her, kiss her or even get close to her. You will take her to the mall, buy her pizza and a Coke, sit across the table from her, talk about school, studying, and going to college; then you'll bring her back home and leave."

"Dude, that's, like, so boring."

"Exactly. You'll be boring or we'll pay you a visit, and it's gonna be ugly."

"Dude, can I, like, hold her hand?"

"Not even for a second. Remember, we are watching your every move."

"What if, like, I say no way?"

Ali held up his fork, "Then you say hello to my friend, the widow maker."

"You call your fork 'window maker'?" Billy asked.

"The widow maker, not 'window maker,' you dumbass," Ali replied.

"You can kill with a fork?"

"I'm a trained assassin. I can turn any ordinary household item into a deadly weapon."

"Far out, dude. Like, can you kill with a saltshaker?" Billy asked.

"That's my specialty. I can show you if you'd like a demo."

"Easy, dude. I totally believe you," Billy said.

Billy's smell of urine was stinking up the car and I needed to end this as soon as possible. "So listen up. You'll ask her out tomorrow and pick her up this Friday," I said.

"I got band practice on Friday."

"Do you think Saddam gives two hoots about your band practice?"

"Cool, man. Whatever Saddam says," Billy said while jumping out of the car.

Ali moved up to the front seat. We removed our head scarves, avoiding eye contact. I felt terrible for doing this to Billy, and I think Ali felt the same way, too.

"Anything else?" Ali asked.

"No, that should do."

"You need to stop doing this."

"I know. I'm a horrible person. What can I say?"

"No. You're just confused like the rest of us. You don't know what's good for your kids. Nobody does."

I thanked Ali for participating in my idiotic games and asked him to join me for dinner someday. He said that he would.

My daughter came home the next day, looking all happy. I hadn't seen her this cheerful since the last time Billy had asked her out.

"Dad, guess what. Billy, the dreamy guy at school, asked me out. I'm so happy."

"Good for you."

My daughter took a few steps back and stared at me. "Who are you and what did you do to my father?"

"Hey, hope you have a good time," I said.

"You're letting me go on a date?"

"Sure, I trust you. Enjoy."

"Dad, you are the coolest."

It's amazing how you become cool in the eyes of your children once you tell them what they want to hear. My daughter got her way and I became the coolest dad in the whole wide world. Now if I had said no, I would have been the worst dad ever. I'm beginning to learn this game.

Billy showed up at the door at exactly six o'clock. He actually looked presentable. His hair was combed back, he was wearing khaki pants and a long-sleeved shirt. I opened the door and let him in. Since Billy had never seen my face during his ordeal, he could not connect the dots.

"Hi, I'm here to pick up Saddam's daughter," Billy said while shaking hands.

"Let's keep that piece of information down low."

"Hey man, it's cool. So, like, who are you?"

"I'm the housekeeper, and sometimes referred to as Dad."

"Oh, I got you."

"Now, I assume you have received your instructions," I said.

"Oh, yes, sir, I know what to do. You can count on me."

"Good."

My daughter ran downstairs and said hello to Billy with a grin that started at one ear and ended somewhere in the vicinity of the other ear. Poor Billy stepped back like my daughter had some sort of contagious disease. I liked what I saw. This was going to work out just fine. Billy was scared of my daughter and that's exactly what I was shooting for.

As my daughter and Billy were leaving the house, I grabbed Billy's shoulder and whispered in his ear. "Remember, Saddam has eyes everywhere."

"Oh, dude, you don't have to tell me."

My daughter got back her popularity at school, and Billy became a legend for daring to date Saddam's daughter. He left the band since he couldn't practice on Fridays and his grades started to improve. Billy also began reading about Middle Eastern culture, which was something I did not expect from a punk rocker. I soon realized that my fears were baseless. My daughter's character was so strong that she not only did not get influenced by Billy, she actually reshaped Billy's personality in a positive way.

Billy removed the piercing and stopped his monthly visits to the neighborhood tattoo parlor. He started hanging around with kids who had a vocabulary of more than fifty words, participated in the school's drama classes and showed an amazing knack for Shakespeare. Billy, who had been voted "most likely to finish high school at age thirty" became a straight-A student and received a scholarship to a very good college on the West Coast.

Billy and my daughter still talk. I learned two very valuable lessons from my encounters with Billy: first, I should trust my children because they are much smarter than I; and second, it's a good idea to cover your face when committing a felony.

11. The Nose Job

MY FRIEND ALI *THE NOSE*, who helped with my daughter's dating situation, called to say hi and see how things were going with her and me. I told him that every day is a struggle to keep her away from teens' daily distractions, but over all, things were going fine. Ali told me that he had good news. "I'm finally going to get a nose job."

Normally I would have protested such a display of male narcissism. The way I see it, if a woman wants plastic surgery done, more power to her. I'm all for symmetrically enhanced bodies roaming the earth, and I love to watch women with perfect features blessing me and the rest of the world with their presence. But the idea of plastic surgery for guys is a little too much for me to handle. However, in Ali's case, I was all for it.

Ali's body stopped growing at the age of nineteen. However, his nose developed a mind of its own and refused to stop growing. He looked as if his nose was on steroids while the rest of his body suffered from malnutrition. His nose not only continued growing at an unimaginable pace, it defied all laws of physics, gravity and anatomy.

When Ali walked into a room, he didn't light up the room, he actually blocked the light. When he was younger, Ali's nose grew large but straight. When he became a bit older, however, his nose decided to make a left turn to check out the view. Growing tired of the view on the left side, his nose took another detour and grew to the right for some fresh air.

While all that twisting and turning were taking place, a strange bump appeared on top of his nose that resembled a golf ball. His nostrils, by far, were the most frightening. They were huge, deep and dark. You couldn't help but wonder if your long-lost TV remote control might be found in there. They looked like two large caves separated by human flesh. You wouldn't dare come close to them for fear of getting sucked in.

Extremely self-conscious of his massive (facial) organ, Ali has been in touch with an Iraqi plastic surgeon in Beverly Hills. The surgeon is credited with beautifying colossal facial features at a reasonable price of only $3,000. He is Western-educated and, according to Ali, performs a number of nose jobs per day with impressive success and high customer satisfaction. If Ali wanted to do the surgery with any other surgeon, he would have to cough up at least $6,000.

Naturally he was very excited about the whole experience. And I was happy for him. A little facial rearrangement would definitely make him look different, maybe even handsome. But there was a little problem: the Iraqi surgeon had gone back to his homeland to help with the reconstruction of his country after the U.S. invasion. The surgeon had opened shop at a hospital in Baghdad and was mostly treating Iraqis with injuries caused by bomb blasts and gunshot wounds.

But Ali looked at this development as a great opportunity to knock another $1,000 off the original price of the surgery.

"So you're going to Iraq to get a nose job?" I asked Ali.

"Yes, I am. I know there is a war and it's dangerous, but I contacted the surgeon, and he assured me that he would have no problem operating on me in Baghdad."

"Do you understand you can get your ass killed over there?" I said.

"It's not as bad as they show it on TV; I'll be just fine."

"You must be absolutely out of your mind," I said.

"Hey, this is important to me. I gotta lose this nose, and you can't beat the price."

"Yeah, you might end up losing more than your nose, like, your entire head."

"It's complicated. There is more to this than you think. But my mind is made up," Ali said. "I'm going to Baghdad."

The night before his departure, Ali stopped by my place to say goodbye. He told me of his idea to send emails during his stay and report on his progress. I thought it was an excellent idea and encouraged him to write as often as he possibly could.

Date: Thu, 12 Feb 04 09:20AM MDT
From: Ali
To: big daddy
Subject: Hi

Hi,

I made it to Baghdad. The place is a mess. I went to see the plastic surgeon. He examined my nose and made all kinds of strange humming sounds. I didn't quite understand his facial expressions either. He sat down at his desk and told me he would charge $4,000 to perform the surgery. I jumped out of my chair. I reminded him of our agreement over the phone on a $2,000 fee. He laughed and said, "Habibi, I charge $2,000 for a normal nose job. This is more like decapitating an elephant. Nobody in the U.S. would touch that thing for less than $6,000. I am actually doing you a favor."

I figured, what the heck. I am here and might as well do it and get it over with. My surgery is scheduled for tomorrow. I am very excited. I can't wait to start my new life.

Date: Fri, 13 Feb 04 12:30AM MDT
From: Ali
To: big daddy

Subject: Didn't happen.

Hi,

I was on my way to the hospital and a bomb blew up just a mile away from the hospital. They had all the streets shut down. I had no choice but to go back to my hotel. I contacted the surgeon and rescheduled the surgery for tomorrow. I have not been able to get much sleep because there is so much shooting here at night. I'll write later.

Date: Tue, 17 Feb 04 12:30AM MDT
From: Ali
To: big daddy
Subject: made it.

Hi,

The surgery took a long time. The electricity was cut off in the middle of the surgery and since the hospital doesn't have any generators, the surgeon had to continue the surgery with a flashlight. The anesthesiologist also ran out of supplies, and he ended up knocking me in the head several times to keep me under. I have a pounding headache.

Anyway, I looked at myself in the mirror this morning and I was horrified. I have tape stuck to my nose so I am not sure what my nose looks like at the moment. But, my face is so swollen, it looks like a huge watermelon. The surgeon was very happy with the operation. He told me that my nose would soon look like a work of art!! I was a bit concerned about the surgery taking place in the dark but the surgeon was optimistic.

I am going in tomorrow for the final checkup and to remove the tape. I got to go now. I need to take some painkillers. I will write later.

Date: Wed, 18 Feb 04 10:20AM MDT
From: Ali
To: big daddy
Subject: didn't make it.

Hi,

I couldn't go back to the hospital for a checkup. Another bomb blew up a mile from the hospital and they closed all the streets. I'm beginning to dislike this place.

Date: Thu, 19 Feb 04 10:20AM MDT
From: Ali
To: big daddy
Subject: What the hell...

Hi,

They removed the tape this morning. The surgeon went overboard with the nose reduction. I am not sure what the hell he was thinking. My nose is the size of a freakin' peanut. It's so small, it looks ridiculous. My nostrils are like two tiny holes now. I can hardly breathe. I think the lack of adequate lighting might have contributed to the results. My face is swollen like hell. I look like a freak. I'm gonna kill these assholes.

Date: Thu, 26 Feb 04 08:20AM MDT
From: Ali
To: big daddy
Subject: Depressed.

I'm depressed. I need to get out of here. A week has passed since my surgery and I still don't recognize myself. My face is badly swollen and the nose.... What nose? You can't even see a nose. I look as if I was in the ring with Mike Tyson and he not only kicked my ass but nailed my nose inside my face.

People here mistake me for an Iraqi prisoner who has just been released from Abu Gharaib prison. The surgeon does not return my calls. I think the phone lines have been blown up. I've not been able to sleep at night. I'm flying out tomorrow. I'll see you in a few days. I'm warning you. You probably won't even recognize me.

Date: Sun, 29 Feb 04 11:00AM MDT
From: Ali
To: big daddy
Subject: still here

Hi,

Yes, I am still in Iraq. I ran into problems at the airport. As I was going through customs I handed my passport to a military intelligence agent. The agent threw the passport back at me and yelled, "Do you think I'm stupid; this isn't you. Who the hell do you think you are, coming here with someone else's passport? This is a criminal offense. I'm going to turn you in to the coalition authorities." He continued, "Couldn't you at least use somebody's passport with a smaller nose?"

I explained to the agent that I was recovering from a horrendous nose job. That's why I didn't look anything like my pictures. The agent said, "You came to Baghdad to get a nose job in middle of the war?! What kind of idiot would do something like that?"

I have been charged with falsifying documents, aiding insurgents, and attempting to enter American soil for terrorist activities. I'm currently scheduled to appear before the military court to argue my case.

To make matters worse, my plastic surgeon has fled the country due to some lawsuits brought against him by the hospital he was working at. It turned out that he had been stealing money from the hospital and as a result he has destroyed all medical records and evidence. Therefore, I am unable to prove that I had the surgery. I think I will be here for a while. I am beginning to think this whole thing was a big mistake. I must go take some more pain-killers. I don't feel like writing anymore. I just want my old self back.

That didn't make any sense. They must have really screwed up his nose; otherwise I see no reason why he shouldn't be able to leave Iraq. I mean, how bad could it be? I wish there were some way I could contact Ali but he left no address or phone number that I could use to reach him. I called several big hospitals in Baghdad but none had any record of Ali ever visiting them. I also contacted a number of large hotels in Baghdad, with no luck.

I finally decided to call Ali's father. He lived only a few blocks from my house. I was hoping he could shed some light on Ali's strange disappearance.

"Hi, I'm a friend of Ali," I told Ali's father on the phone. "Do you know where your son is?"

"He is in hell, I hope, that bastard," Ali's father said.

"Excuse me?"

"You're all a bunch of gay bastards. I hope you all go to hell."

"Hey, what the heck is your problem? I just wanted to know if Ali was okay," I said.

"I don't care. I don't wanna see him or any of his fag friends. I have no son."

"Hey, take it easy; he might need our help."

"I don't give a crap what he needs. As Allah is my witness, he is dead as far as I'm concerned."

Ali's father slammed the handset back on the phone and hung up on me. I guess he was really disappointed with Ali getting a nose job. Was the man overreacting or what? I understand that some traditional Middle Eastern parents can be a little overprotective when it comes to their sons' experimentation with plastic surgery, but Ali's father was surely missing a few wires upstairs.

A few months passed and I didn't hear any news from Ali. My conscience was clear; I had done everything I could to locate him. One day I came home, checked my answering machine and there it was, Ali's voice, "Hi, it's me, Ali. Sorry it took me so long to call you. I'm back in town and doing fine. Let's get together at the old hangout for a drink. I got a lot to tell you."

Ali sounded suspiciously strange. There was something unfamiliar about his voice. It must have been my answering machine. He sounded happy! I figured he was either on some heavy doses of antidepressant medication, or he had completely lost it.

I went to the old hangout, late as always, and sat at a table in the bar. There was no sign of Ali, which was surprising since he was a very punctual man. I ordered a drink, lit up a cigarette and relaxed my body against the seat. I was curious to see how Ali's nose turned out. I kept telling myself, don't stare at his nose. I was dying to know what happened to him. Did he end up in Abu Gharaib prison? Was he forced to do the naked human pyramid? There was so much to talk about.

I felt someone approaching me from behind. The heavy smell of a woman's perfume filled the air. I turned back and saw a redhead standing behind me.

"Hi. Can I cadge a cigarette from you?" the redhead asked.

"Sure."

I gave her a cigarette and the lighter. She sat down at my table. I'm thinking this chick is trying to pick me up. That was the first time I was ever approached by a woman. It must have been my new haircut. The redhead was sort of average-looking, slim and tall. I figured she can keep me entertained until Ali shows up, and if Ali doesn't show, oh well. But there was something very familiar about her. I was sure that I had seen her somewhere.

"Have we met?" I asked. "You look familiar."

"Maybe."

"Have we met at the gym?"

"No," she answered

"PTA meeting?"

"No."

"Are you a friend of my ex-wife?" I asked.

"No."

"Oh, I know. I met you at my father-in-law's funeral."

"Yes, I was there."

"What's your name?"

"Alison," she answered, "but my friends call me Ali."

I fell off my chair. No way! No freakin' way!!! This is not happening!

"What the fuck?"

"Hi, it's me."

"Is this some kind of a joke?" I asked.

"No, it's not a joke."

I pulled back my chair. I started breathing heavily. The hair on the back of my neck stood up. My chest got tight and I was sure I was having a heart attack. My buddy, Ali, was sitting in front me except he—or in this case, she—didn't look anything like himself.

"What the hell are you doing dressing like a woman?" I asked Ali.

"I want to apologize. I should've given you a warning."

"What are you doing? Am I on candid camera?" I asked, looking around.

Ali pulled his seat closer. I jumped out of my seat and stepped away from the table. This was the most uncomfortable situation I'd ever been in my whole life.

"Please sit down. I'm not going to bite," Ali said.

"I don't wanna sit down. I wanna leave."

"Listen, just give me two minutes. Let me explain," Ali said.

"How can you possibly explain this? You are a woman. What the hell, man?"

"I've always been a woman. I was a woman trapped in a man's body," Ali said.

"Uh, give me a break," I cried out.

"I'm serious. I always acted like a man because I was ashamed of my feelings. I'm a Middle Eastern man. Imagine the shame I could've brought to my family. But I just couldn't do it anymore. I tried but it just didn't work for me. Please understand."

My pal, Ali, is sitting in front of me in a dress, a wig, and stockings, with a face full of makeup and voice like a little twelve-year-old girl and he is asking me to "please understand."

"Understand what?" I said. "Is this some kind of rebellion against your old man? Don't you think you're a little too old for this?"

"This is me. What you see here is who I really am."

"Do you like men?" I asked.

"Yes."

"What the hell. A little warning would've been nice. I bent over a bunch of times in front of you. I have been naked in front of you, for God's sake. I feel so used, man. How could you do this to me?"

"It's okay, you're not my type," Ali said

"Excuse me? What's wrong with me?"

"You are a good man, but you just don't have that spark."

"Spark? I have more spark than you can ever handle," I replied.

"Sorry," Ali said.

"What the hell am I saying? You're a cross-dresser, a man-she."

"Actually, it's a little more complicated. I had the operation."

"The what?"

"I had the sex change operation while I was in Iraq. I feel terrible for lying to everybody, but I had to," Ali said.

"So you went all the way to Iraq to get your balls cut off?"

"That and some other operations."

"What about the emails? What about the nose job?" I asked.

"My emails were sort of true. I did get a nose job plus some other facial modification, breast augmentation, liposuction, buttocks implants, tummy tuck and, of course, the removal of some unwanted parts."

"Oh, man, why are you telling me all this?"

"Because I don't wanna pretend anymore. I wanna be who I am for once, and I want my friends to accept me for who I am."

"What about the thing at the airport?" I asked.

"That actually was true. I was not able to leave Iraq since my passport had the letter M in front of 'sex.'"

"I'm getting sick. I need some fresh air," I said.

"I understand; it takes time to get used to it."

"Get used to it? Who are you? I don't even know you. Where is my friend, Ali?"

"I'm your friend, Ali. But please call me Alison."

"Oh, don't do that, dude. I gotta go."

"Please, I just wanna be friends," Ali said.

"I don't know about that. I need time to think this over," I said, walking away from the table.

I was surprised to see myself so out of control, dealing with Ali's new image. We are talking serious emotional leakage. I don't know why but my body was exhausted, and I felt a strange numbness on the right side of my face. I consider myself an open-minded person when it comes to other people's choice of lifestyle. I guess we are all open-minded so long as we don't have to deal with difficult issues. But this experience with Ali or Alison showed me how difficult it is to deal with unorthodox circumstances, especially when they involve someone you have history with.

Ali was a great friend, my partner in crime and my confidant. But Alison was someone I didn't know anything about, and I just couldn't picture myself sitting at a bar with her, drinking beer and discussing a hundred different ways to get women into bed. Another problem with Alison was that he was a she, and like many other men out there, I'm incapable of being friends with women. It can't be done, not a chance. Every man out there who claims to be only friends with women is either gay or he is selling something. I decided that I had enough complex issues in my life at the moment, and I just had to let this one go for now. No point in dealing with unwanted issues today when there is always tomorrow.

12. Here Comes Grandpa

HAVING LEFT IRAN IN MY EARLY TEENS, I've kept precious memories of the family I left behind. Memories that have become foggy as the years have gone by. Every year I must dig deeper in my mind to remember certain events or certain people that I've not seen or heard from for close to thirty years. But one person who always stood out in my mind was Grandpa. A no-nonsense, mighty strong man with a broad chest and biceps the size of an oak tree, Grandpa was a larger-than-life figure that commanded respect and admiration from friends and foes. I remember walking down the streets of Tehran in the summertime by his side and seeing firsthand the level of reverence he received from people who knew him. The man was known by everyone. Grandpa was also known for his way with the ladies. He was a lady-killer, a charmer and a huge womanizer—trades that I certainly did not inherit from him.

Grandpa was my security blanket. Everything was all right as long as he was around. I talked to him often after I left for the U.S., but we eventually grew apart and our communications came to a sudden halt. But one day, after a few years of no contact, Grandpa called me. I was surprised.

I was having myself a beautiful night—sitting at home, chilling with my ex-wife, who was still my wife at the time, watching Jerry Springer. This one was my favorite episode where this large girl was having an affair with her seventy-year-old father-in-law, and at the same time her husband was doing the nasty with her grandma.

As things started heating up and the large girl was just about ready to confront her husband, and her father-in-law was beating the hell out of her grandma, my phone rang. I couldn't believe it. Whoever interrupts my Jerry shall be punished. I picked up the phone violently and shouted, "WHAT?"

I heard static followed by a short beep and a voice that sounded like it was coming from another galaxy.

"Hello, how the heck are you, my boy?" the voice said.

"I was fine till you called; who's this?"

"Pedarsag (father dog), you don't recognize me? Shame on you."

"Who is this?" I asked.

"Pedarsookhteh (father burned), it's your Grandpa."

"Hey, Grandpa," I replied. "What a great surprise. How are you?"

"Listen, I need to make this quick. I'm calling from a public phone in Tehran, paying arms and legs for this call. Baba joon, I am down on my luck, things have not been going well lately, life is difficult here. It's stressful and unpredictable, so expensive and hectic. You have to run around all day to get this and get that; affects a man's well-being and hits the pocket hard, you know? I have a problem you can solve, a personal favor."

"What can I do for you?" I asked.

"Send me the pill."

"Excuse me? The what?"

"The pill, you know—the blue pill."

"Advil?"

"Not Advil. The pill, the one that makes the dead man rise from the coffin."

"Dead? Don't tell me you've got cancer," I said.

"I don't have cancer, you moron. Listen, there are people standing behind me waiting to use the phone. They are listening. I can't say the name of the pill out loud. I need the pill that makes the rusty old cannon fire again, you know—the one that put Casanova back in business, the one that makes your soldier stand up and salute during the national anthem."

"What the hell are you talking about? What cannon? What national anthem?"

"Are you dumb?" he shouted. "I need the pill that turns the snake to a cane, the pill that brings the worm out of its hole, the blue pill that made the Hunchback of Notre Dame stand up straight and sing like a soprano."

"Oh, I get it. You need supplements with vitamins for your back pain."

"Idiot, I don't need supplements. Listen to me. The wife has not been happy with the performance. I need the pill that turns a Yugo into a BMW."

"I'm sorry. You keep getting cut off," I yelled. "Anyway, to improve the performance of your Yugo, I recommend using unleaded gasoline with performance spark plugs."

"Grandson, I wish you were standing here right now so I could smash this handset on your head. Concentrate. I need the pill that puts the flag back on the pole, the pill that makes the old man die of a heart attack with a smile on his face."

"Grandpa, all you have to do is take one aspirin a day to prevent heart attacks."

"What a frickin idiot." Grandpa yelled, and hung up the phone.

"Hello, Grandpa, hello?"

I went back to watching my show.

"Who was it?" my wife asked.

"It was my Grandpa calling from Iran; dirty old man wanted Viagra."

So you can imagine how excited I was to hear that Grandpa was finally coming to visit. I couldn't wait to have my kids meet their great grandpa. I told them so many good things about him. Seeing the mighty man of the family in person would boost their morale and bring them closer to their roots, which was something they needed to experience. Grandpa also needed to meet his great grandchildren before he said goodbye and moved into his six-by-two vacation home. This meeting was way overdue.

I went to my parents' house to see Grandpa and the kids came with me. I walked into the room and almost fainted. I was shocked to see how old Grandpa had gotten. The mighty athletic man of the family, who resembled Hercules in his heyday, looked small, fragile and bent out of shape. I guess age does that to you.

"Hey, Grandpa, how you doing?" I said.

"What?"

"How are you?" I yelled.

"How am I? I'm wearing a diaper and I can't feel my legs. How do you think I am?"

"You look good, Grandpa."

"Ah, bullshit. I look like crap and I feel like crap."

"I've missed you, man," I said.

"You missed the old me. The new me, you can't stand. I guarantee you."

"What's the problem, Grandpa?"

"Everything. Everything hurts and nothing works. All the pipes that are supposed to be open are clogged, and all the pipes that are supposed to be closed are leaking."

"Well, maybe we should go see a doctor, open up the old hood, look at the engine, see how things are hanging. Let's find out what's up."

"I tell you this much: everything is hanging and nothing is up."

"Come on, Grandpa, I'll take you to see a doctor. You and me like in the good old days."

"A doctor? I have never been to a doctor in my life, and I sure as hell ain't gonna start now."

"Grandpa, you're not as strong as you used to be."

"Hell, no. I don't need no doctor; I need women. I need young, beautiful women that make a man young. If you had sent me the blue pills, I would have been okay now."

"Don't start that again," I said

"I need the pills. I need to get my hands on the damn pills."

"You don't need Viagra."

"Yes, I do."

"Aren't you a little too old for that?" I asked.

"Old? All my friends are doing it. I'm missing out."

"You are ninety. Viagra is gonna kill you."

"So what? You call this livin'?" Grandpa said.

"Okay, you want the blue pills? You got it, but first you gotta go for a checkup. If you're fit, then I'll ask the doctor to give you the pills."

That was convincing enough for Grandpa to go see a doctor. Once he knew that the doctor could prescribe Viagra, he was ready for his first checkup ever.

I took him to the doctor. Grandpa seemed nervous. The doctor asked me to stay in the waiting room while he examined Grandpa in his office. I settled into a chair, grabbed a magazine, relaxed and started flipping pages. It was a good day and I was proud of myself. I was doing a good thing and it felt right. For all the years that Grandpa took care of me, it was now my turn to return the favor.

A few minutes passed and all of sudden, I heard commotion coming from the doctor's examination room. I dropped the magazine and ran inside. I opened the door and found Grandpa swinging his cane in the air, chasing the doctor around the room.

"You son of a bitch, how dare you," Grandpa shouted.

"What the hell's going on here?" I asked Grandpa.

"What is going on?" Grandpa said. "I tell you what's going on. This son of a bitch attacked my manhood. I'll kill him."

"Attacked your manhood? What you talking about?" I asked.

"Yes, a surprise attack from behind, an ambush, a finger rape." Grandpa said.

"Finger rape?"

The chase continued. Grandpa was knocking supplies off the tables while swinging his cane carelessly at the doctor. The poor doctor was trying desperately to find cover behind the furniture. I grabbed Grandpa and forced him to sit down. I turned to the doctor and asked, "Doc, what did you do to him?"

"Nothing," the doctor said. "I was checking the gentleman's prostate. As soon as I inserted the finger, the man went wild. I think he wants to kill me."

So it turns out that the doctor was doing his finger test to check Grandpa's prostate, and Grandpa, not knowing what the doctor was doing, completely misunderstood the action.

I entirely forgot that sticking a finger in a Middle Eastern man's behind is the ultimate form of insult. Grandpa, being a traditional Middle Eastern man, was devastated by the gesture and wanted nothing short of blood to restore his honor.

"Grandpa, calm down. The doctor was only checking your prostate for cancer. That's what doctors do."

"Shut up. For ninety years I protected my reputation. I didn't allow no one near the crack. There were attacks from certain elements, but I fought to preserve the sanctity and the sacredness of my manhood. Then I let my guard down for a moment, and this so-called doctor takes advantage."

"Grandpa, he is a physician, for God's sake."

"I don't care. He violated the temple of nobility."

"What? You call your ass 'the temple of nobility'?"

"Yes, I do. It's meant to be an exit, not an entrance," Grandpa said.

"Grandpa, listen to me. It's okay. It's just a routine checkup. I myself get a physical every year, and among other things, the good doctor checks my prostate by doing what he did to you."

"So you're telling me that every year you come to this idiot, bend over, and let him stick his finger in your crack?"

"Yes," I replied.

"I always knew you were gay."

Grandpa got up and walked out of the examination room. I followed him outside. "Hey, you want Viagra, you gotta let him finish his exam," I said.

"The hell with you and Viagra. I'm outta here."

I felt sorry for Grandpa. After that incident, the man sat in a chair in his room and stared blankly at the wall. He was a broken man. He not only didn't get his blue pills, his so-called temple of nobility had been ambushed and penetrated viciously. Grandpa was not the type of man who took his honor lightly. I had to do something to get his mind off the subject, so I asked him if there was anything I could do to cheer him up.

"Yes, there is," Grandpa said. "Get me the damn pills and take me to Las Vegas so I can feel young again."

"Would you please get off that subject? I cannot get you the pills. It's not like I can go to a drugstore and pick them off the shelf."

"Why not?"

"Because I must have a doctor's prescription, and the doctor has to check your heart before giving you the pills."

"Oh, I didn't know my heart was in my ass."

"Grandpa, let it go."

"I just wanna feel like a real man again. Is that too much to ask?"

That broke my heart. I saw my future in front of me. The cruelty of nature. You go about your business all capable and healthy, having no idea that someday you'll consider getting from your bedroom to the kitchen in twenty minutes a major accomplishment. A few drops of pee make your day, and only ten visits to bathroom at night bring a smile to your face. God sure knows how to treat people with dignity in their golden years.

Grandpa, the ladies man who in his younger years melted the heart of every woman he laid eyes on, was now longing for a moment of his past glories. The man who flamed jealousy and resentment in every married man's soul for the attention he received from women of all ages and forms, was now a frail man, sitting in a chair, dreaming of his lost greatness.

Maybe he just wanted a small taste of a moment of his past victories. Maybe he just wanted to see his little friend stand up and say hi for old time's sake. And maybe he needed to see his fountain of youth spew one last time. I had to get him the pills.

I visited a doctor friend of mine and asked him for some Viagra samples. I intentionally left out a small detail. I obviously didn't want to tell him that I needed the pills for a ninety-year-old man.

"I'm happy for you. It's about time you got back in the saddle," my doctor friend said.

"Actually, they're for a friend."

"Yeah, they all say that."

"No, really," I said.

"Okay, fine. Just remember, erectile dysfunction is nothing to be ashamed of."

"My erection is doing just fine; thanks for asking."

"It can happen to guys younger than you. You know?"

"Well, that makes me feel much better; but seriously, they're for someone else," I said.

"It's okay. Millions of men have that problem. It's natural to feel self-conscious. I myself am a user."

"I really didn't have to know that," I said.

"And always practice safe sex."

"I'll try to remember that," I said.

"Remember, you have a problem and you're doing something about it. That takes courage."

"Yeah, that's me. I'm all about courage."

"Here it is," my doctor friend said, handing me the samples. "These pills will satisfy your every desire."

"I doubt it," I said. "Unless they can paint my house and wash the dishes."

So there we were on a road trip: me, Grandpa, and two packs of Viagra riding in my pimpmobile on the way to the brothels of Nevada. I had never seen Grandpa so happy. He was breathless with anticipation, and I, on the other hand, was worried sick about the outcome of this trip. I had killed my father-in-law and that was okay, but killing Grandpa—my childhood hero—was something I couldn't deal with.

As I was pulling into the parking lot of the finest brothel in Nevada, Grandpa jumped out and ran inside before the car came to a complete halt. I'd never seen a ninety-year-old man move so fast.

I went inside and found Grandpa facing a lineup of beautiful young women in cheap erotic customs, phony smiles and fake breasts. The place looked like a large house with living room, kitchen, family room and a small bar in the corner. I guess the idea is to make you feel at home. The smell of cigarette smoke and discount perfumes was overwhelming.

I personally have tremendous respect for the business of prostitution. Prostitution does the society good. Prostitution is one of few professions that engage in the business of aggression control and stress management, which is an essential component of every healthy society. A country full of horny people is unpredictable and dysfunctional. You never know what's going to happen next. A horny person does not make rational decisions and cannot be trusted. A horny person is always on the edge. Some of the most devastating wars started when decisions were made while leaders were horny. That's why we never faced the danger of war while Bill Clinton was in office and Monica Lewinsky should be awarded the Nobel Peace Prize for keeping the world a safer place.

Prostitution is a sensational business model. Where else can you find the same stinky, beat-up, overused product being sold over and over again for a premium price? That, my friends, is an ingenious marketing strategy, which should be taught in business schools all over the world. Prostitution brings honesty back into casual relationships and frees the human race from pretentious protocols. You don't take a prostitute out to dinner, buy her flowers, or lie to get her into your bedroom. You don't have to impress a prostitute with your money, car, or house, and you certainly don't have to compete for her affection. You pay, do your thing, and get the hell out; no attachments, no promises, no problem.

Grandpa was standing there staring at the goods like he had just died and gone to heaven. He was speechless.

"Okay, Grandpa, here we are; go ahead and pick one," I said.

"Just one?"

"What do you mean, just one? How many do you want?"

"We are here, might as well pick two. You know how girls are; they might get jealous if I only picked one."

I forgot I was dealing with an Iranian man.

"Okay, pick two."

Grandpa pulled out his bifocals and examined the commodities carefully. He then pointed at two fine ladies in the lineup with his cane. The two ladies walked out of the lineup and grabbed Grandpa's arms on each side.

"Give me my pills," Grandpa said.

"Okay, take just one. Get it?"

"But I have two girls here."

"No matter how many girls you got there, just one pill."

"Okay, get me some water and don't wait up for me."

Grandpa fiercely swallowed the blue pill and walked down a long dark corridor, hand-in-hand with the two working girls. I went back to the car and waited there. You know you have reached the lowest point in your life when you find yourself pandering for your own grandfather. And the strange thing is: Grandpa was doing the deed and I was the one who had the butterflies.

An hour passed and there was no sign of Grandpa. I leaned the car seat back and closed my eyes. I heard someone knocking on the side window. I opened my eyes with a start and found the manager of the establishment looking at me through the window. I got out of the car in a hurry. "What's going on?"

"The old man requested two additional girls and he wants his pills," the manager said.

"Come again?"

"Your grandpa needs reinforcements."

"Two additional girls?"

"Yes, sir. The man is a machine," the manager said.

"Is he okay?" I asked.

"From what I hear, he's never been better."

"He needs another pill?"

"Yeah. I guess his balloon has deflated."

I reluctantly gave the manager another Viagra and went back into the car. Grandpa's orgy was costing me a fortune, but it was all worth it as long as he was happy. I relaxed my body against the seat, closed my eyes and fell sleep.

Another hour passed and there was no sign of Grandpa. I got out of the car, stretched my legs and pulled out a cigarette. The door to the house swung open wildly and the manager ran out. "Sir, we've got a problem."

"What?"

"Please come with me," the manager said.

I ran inside the house and followed the manager through the dark corridors into a bedroom. Grandpa was lying on a bed motionless, surrounded by six working girls. One of the girls was banging on Grandpa's chest, and another girl was giving him mouth-to-mouth.

"What happened here?" I asked.

"Well, the old man requested two additional girls," the manager said. "I came out to ask for your permission but you were sleeping in the car, so I figured what the heck, it's on me."

"He was in the room with six girls?" I asked.

"Yeah, the old man has quite an appetite. He also requested a bottle of champagne. He wouldn't take no for an answer. He started chasing the girls around the room. Then his heart stopped."

"Are you crazy? You put a ninety-year-old man on Viagra in a room with six young women and a bottle of champagne and expected him to live through it?"

"Well, we're lucky because one of the girls here is also a part-time nurse," the manager explained.

The chest banging and CPR continued. I held my breath. This was not going to look good and the family would definitely kill me. How could I explain this to my grandma? One look at the stiff body and she would know exactly what had happened. And what am I going to tell my kids? I took Grandpa to a whorehouse and killed him? Yeah, I'm some kind of a role model for my kids.

All of a sudden, Grandpa took a deep breath and opened his eyes. The lady who was banging on his chest stopped and took his pulse.

"Is he gonna be okay?" I asked the nurse/hooker/paramedic lady.

"Yeah, he'll live," she answered.

"Call nine-one-one." I yelled

"They're on their way," the manager answered.

I held Grandpa's hand and whispered in his ear, "You okay?"

"Never better, should have seen me, I was brilliant. If only the goddamn heart could keep up with the rest of me."

"Six girls? Are you out of your mind?" I asked.

"Sure. If you gonna go, go in style."

"Was it worth dying for?"

"Absolutely. I saw an old friend; he was smiling. Hadn't seen him this happy in years. I was planning on dying like a man and what better place than in the arms of six beautiful ladies?" Grandpa said as he broke down in tears.

Grandpa was transferred to a hospital in Las Vegas. The story circulated through the hospital, and doctors and nurses stopped by to see the legend in the flesh. My grandpa became a celebrity and even some hospital staff asked for his autograph. The ladies at the brothel stopped by frequently at the hospital and visited him. They even named Grandpa "the sword man of the Persian empire."

Grandpa eventually recovered and went back to Iran. I came close to getting another family member killed in a freak accident, but this one surprisingly worked out at the end. Grandpa's adventures and hospital bills cost me my children's college fund, but that's okay. The memories of Grandpa's visit to America will last me forever. So will the payments.

13 The Last Wish

AMONG THE LONG LIST OF MY MISTAKES in life, the one I regret the most by far is losing my wife. What can I say? I missed her. I missed her bitching, her silent treatments, her stupid family and her occasional smiles. Actually her smiles were so sporadic I can vividly recall every single one of them. But I loved her, and regardless of her conduct and negative outlook on life, in my mind, she was still my wife.

When you get to a certain age, bouncing back from failures becomes more and more difficult. You begin taking negative outcomes personally and don't stomach disappointments as well as you used to in your younger days. I thought about the ex all the time, and the more I thought about her, the more I realized that life was not much fun without her. I guess we're all masochists by nature in some ways. Women who go through unbearable pregnancies desire more children after a year or two, athletes who suffer life-threatening injuries on the field can't wait to return to action, people who spend a lifetime complaining about work get bored of retirement after a few months, and I couldn't see myself living another day without my ex-wife, who had brought nothing but pain and agony to my life. So it was clear: I had to get the ex-wife back.

This was a huge challenge since I had burned all my bridges with her, and I was nonexistent as far as she was concerned. But things were not exactly peachy in the ex-wife's neck of the woods. Based on information I gathered from the kids' visits, the ex-wife and the podiatrist boyfriend were not doing so hot. It turned out that the ex-wife was tired of the podiatrist's lack of enthusiasm for leading a bit more exciting life.

The podiatrist boyfriend spent most of his time working and reading, and the ex-wife, who had never worked a day in her life, was mostly left by her lonesome. As in any other relationship, the romance and passion were replaced by practicality, and both sides stopped being polite. The fact that she was not the podiatrist's center of attention did not sit well with her, and she began to think—for the first time in her life—that the whole world might not revolve around her needs.

The problem with divorced women is that they're idealistic. That comes from years of isolation and lack of experience in real life. Divorced women actually think there are men out there who can relate to them. They're under the impression that there are men who are sensitive and considerate. What a bunch of bull.

The ex-wife eventually noticed that men and women do not necessarily relate; they simply coexist for a common cause, which could be financial, emotional, or simply to pass on the genes. She was also shocked to realize that there is no such thing as unconditional love, and at the end of the day, all men are created equal.

This was a rude awakening for the ex. She was not stupid and she started questioning many of her judgments. And best of all, she began to think that I was not as bad as she thought I was. Sure, I farted and burped, I scratched my balls and did stupid things, and I was not emotionally available on short notice and I was ethically challenged, but with all my faults I was never accused of being boring, and there was always something unpredictable happening in our household. Basically, my lack of common sense kept life interesting.

Gathering all this information, I figured it was time to approach the ex and start screwing with her mind. The ultimate objectives were, of course, to get her back, get my life on track, and put my family back together.

I was supposed to drop the kids off at their mother's house. The kids told me that their mother's boyfriend was out of town. This was my chance to get the wheels in motion. I got a nice haircut, shaved, and put on some spiffy clothes. My kids were taken aback by the transformation.

"You got a date, Dad?" My daughter asked.

"Yes, I do."

"Uh, that's why you took a shower?"

"I always take a shower," I answered.

"No, you don't."

I would normally drop the kids at her house and take off. Not today. I was going in to do some damage. So I parked the car and walked to the door with the kids.

"What are you doing, Dad?" my son asked.

"Nothing. Wanna make sure you guys are okay."

"Dad, you're acting weird today," my daughter said.

"Hey, I love you guys, and I wanna make sure you get to your mother's house safe and sound."

"Never did that before," my son said.

"Well, never too late to become a good dad."

"Dad, you trying to come in and hit on mom?" my son asked.

"Oh, shut up."

The ex was shocked to find me on the other side of the door. She froze. "Hey, how are you?" I said.

"What do you want?" she asked.

"Nothing. Been awhile; came to say hi."

The kids pushed their way in and so did I. I have to admit, it was an awkward moment. The ex-wife and I stood in the hallway and looked at each other. I always loved her morning look. There was something sexy about her when she woke up from her usual eleven-hour sleep.

"You look good," the ex said.

"Yeah, been lifting again."

"Wish I had time for that."

"You look nice; you don't need to exercise," I said.

"Why are you flattering me? What do you want?"

The ex-wife stared at me like she was trying to read my mind. She knew I was up to no good, but she couldn't put her finger on it. Okay, here was the plan: since I always scam to get what I want, I figured the best way to get her remotely interested in me again was to make her jealous. That's right. Jealousy was the way to go. Jealousy is the mother of all motivations, a powerful tool, and it works every time.

"Well, you see, I'm actually here to get your opinion on something."

"No," she said.

"Listen, I just need a woman's point of view, that's all."

As expected, I got her attention.

"What is it?"

"Well, I've been seeing this woman, exciting, beautiful, total package. Things are going great, but I sense she wants to move the relationship to the next stage, and I'm not sure how to tell. What are the signs? How can you be sure?"

As soon as I finished my sentence, I saw flames burning in my ex-wife's eyes. This was totally unexpected. I was convinced now that her relationship with the boyfriend was heading south at the speed of light and she was shocked to find my romantic life vibrant and healthy. This was going to be just perfect. She was the type of person who could not bear to see other people happier than her. And on top of that, she visibly still had feelings for me. Score!

"Why are you telling me this?" she said.

"Because you know me the best, and you know women."

"I don't wanna talk about who you sleep with."

"I didn't know you cared so much about who I slept with," I said.

"Well, I don't."

"Okay, whatever, it was good seeing you," I said, and walked confidently out of her house. She stood there and looked as I walked down the driveway and got into my car.

"Hey," the ex said, "who is she?"

"Who is who?"

"The woman, do I know her?"

I got out of the car and walked back to her house. "Pardon?"

"Do I know her?" she asked.

"I don't think so. She is a professional; she doesn't stay home all day," I replied, smiling. Another score. I was on fire.

"I have a right to know who you bring home while my children stay with you."

"Oh, she is a lawyer and the chairwoman of a successful company. I assure you that she will be a great influence on the kids," I said.

The ex was getting jittery now. She was about to blow a gasket. "I'd like to meet her."

"Excuse me?" I said

"I'd like to meet her. You know my boyfriend; I'd like to know your girlfriend. That's only fair," she said.

Busted! She was onto me. This was not a very good development. The ex was too smart to fall for this.

"I don't think she would be comfortable with that," I said.

"Why not?" she asked. "She knows you have kids, right?"

"Of course she does," I answered. "But she is shy."

"Yeah, right. There is no one."

"Yes, there is. You wanna meet her? You got it. Just tell me when and where," I answered.

"Okay, why don't we all meet next week for dinner at the Compass Room? I'll bring my boyfriend."

"Fine."

"Fine."

A pessimist would have been disappointed with the outcome, but I saw this as an opportunity to make my ex-wife even more jealous. However, there was a small problem: where the hell was I going to find a woman that fit the description? I mean there was no way in hell I could meet a woman of great qualities who happened to be a lawyer and a chairwoman of a company in one week. If the ex found out that I was up to my old tricks, she would never, ever talk to me again. However, if I could pull this off, the combination of her compulsive jealousy and lack of a prosperous future with the current boyfriend would draw her back to me.

I pondered obsessively over this predicament for a few days and finally found the solution. I admit that it was not the solution I was hoping for, but I was desperate. So I picked up the phone and dialed.

"Hey, how are you? Long time no talk."

"Hi. I thought you didn't wanna talk to me again," she replied.

"Me? No way. I mean, come on, you and I are pals and I don't abandon my friends."

"That's nice. I'm glad you've come around," Alison said.

That's right folks, Ali *The Nose,* or in this case, Alison the she-male was my solution to this problem. I know what you're thinking. You are thinking that I'm the most unethical man on the face of the earth. True, I might be, but in times of trouble, who can you rely on if not your friends? I understand that I originally didn't want to have anything to do with Alison, but I'm the master of flip-flops, and like many other people out there, I change my stance on issues when it comes to personal gain.

Ali was my buddy and we had some criminal history (Billy, the lover boy). True, Ali is not the man he used to be, but if I'm to pull this scam off, I need Ali by my side.

"So, how is it hanging? Oops, I mean how are you?" I asked.

"Fine. And you?"

"Doing fine. Listen, I'm not gonna beat around the help, I need your bush," I said.

"Excuse me?" Alison said.

"Sorry, what I meant was, I'm not gonna beat around the bush, I need your help."

"Oh, that's why you called? I should've known," Alison said.

"Oh, come on dude, what you gonna do, say no to me?"

"Yes, I refuse to get involved with your tricks anymore. I'm a lady now and I'm going to act like one."

"I know you are a lady," I said. "And that's exactly why I need your help."

Ali paused for few moments. I could hear his mind grinding at hundred miles an hour, trying to figure out the best way to politely get rid of me.

"I'm sorry, I can't," she said.

"I really need your help. It's important, and I promise it will be the last time."

"No."

"Come on, Ali. It's gonna be exciting, like the good old days, two amigos on the run."

"No," she said.

"Fine, I guess that's what happens when they cutoff your balls."

Another long moment of silence followed by heavy breathing. I struck a chord with Ali. I guess deep inside there was still a shred of manliness left in him.

"Do not question my manhood. I might be a woman but I'm still a lot more man than you'll ever be."

"Prove it," I said.

"Fine. What do you want? You want me to put a knife in some poor kid's throat? You got it, let's go," Alison said.

Yeah, baby! Ali *The Nose* was back. What can I say? I've always had this talent to bring out the worst in women. I explained my plans to Ali. I told her that I was planning to get the ex back, and I needed her to act as my sophisticated girlfriend.

"I gotta give it to you," Ali said, "never a dull moment hanging with you."

"What can I say? What I'm missing in intelligence, I somehow make up for with cowardliness."

The stage was set. I asked Ali to buy a nice dress for the occasion, see a cosmetologist, shave, wax and do everything necessary to look as womanly as possible.

I picked up Ali at her apartment. The dress was nice and she looked glamorous. It's amazing what plastic surgery, diet, makeup, and months of hormone therapy can do. He looked exactly like a she and she didn't look anything like a he. Makes you wonder about some women you meet in nightclubs after a few shots of tequila. I started getting nauseated again but I had no choice, except to hold it in.

"Hi," Ali said. "Thanks for picking me up. This is my first date as a woman. It's exciting."

"Whoa, please control your estrogen. This is not a date, okay? This is just a role-play. Don't get any ideas in your head. I only date individuals who are certified as female at a hospital by a qualified doctor immediately after birth."

"Hey, you need me more than I need you," Ali said.

"True, but I'm just setting expectations here."

"All I expect from you is a little respect and friendship."

"And that you'll have so long as there are forty inches' distance between you and me at all times," I said

"Fine. Like I said, you're not my type."

"And thank God for that."

"Screw you."

"C'mon, dude. Don't be shitty."

"Just drive; Okay," Ali said.

This was a strange experience. Ali and I were arguing like husband and wife. What the heck is going on here? When Ali was a he, I could ask him for favors without hesitation. It was a guy thing. You ask your buddy for things, you get things, and you forget about it. With Alison, it felt different. I actually felt like I was using her. There was remorse and reluctance involved. It felt like I was taking advantage of an innocent woman. Even though Alison and Ali were the exact same individual, I felt no bond whatsoever with Alison.

We walked into the restaurant and found the ex and the boyfriend sitting at a table, waiting for us. Knowing my ex-wife's expressions, I immediately knew that she and the boyfriend must have had a huge fight prior to our arrival.

"Hi, all," I said. "I would like you to meet Alison."

Introductions were made and we all sat down at the table. I was watching my ex-wife from the corner of my eyes. She was staring at Ali with a combination of curiosity and resentment.

"Gosh, Alison, you look so familiar," the ex said.

"I get that all the time," Ali said.

"No, really, I could swear I've seen you before," the ex said.

This was entertaining, If only the ex-wife knew Alison was our old family friend Ali.

"Well, you might have seen her in magazines. Being a lawyer and chairwoman of a large company, she's in the news a lot," I said.

"What kind of law do you practice?" the boyfriend asked.

"Corporate law, specializing in sexual harassment," Ali said.

"That sounds pretty boring," the ex said.

"Actually, Alison teaches seminars all over the world about sexual harassment," I said.

"Really," the ex said. "Obviously Alison hasn't looked up the term sexual harassment in a dictionary, because she would've found your picture next to the words."

Ouch. Ex-wife 1, ex-husband 0.

"Actually, I think it is fascinating," the podiatrist said. "I wish my girlfriend, too, would get off her ass and do something interesting for a change."

The torpedo was launched. Let the war begin.

"Actually, the most rewarding part of my day is by far the thrill of running a major corporation," Ali said.

"I bet," the boyfriend said. "It's good to see more and more women getting involved with corporate America, especially women as beautiful as you."

"Oh, you're such a sweet man." Ali said.

"I'm just pointing out the obvious," the boyfriend said.

I couldn't believe my eyes! My ex's boyfriend was hitting on Ali in front of his girlfriend.

"Oh, shut up, you bald-headed freak," the ex said. "You want a corporate America chick? Then get your shit out of my house and go find one."

"No, you shut up, you witch," the boyfriend replied. "I'm sick of you telling me what to do. For someone who doesn't even know how to spell the word employment, you sure know how to manage my life."

"What life?" the ex said. "You need to have one before I can manage it."

"I had a life until I met you," the boyfriend replied.

"Oh, really? You call getting together with a bunch of horny nerds and reading books a life?"

"I love books," Ali said.

"You stay out of this with your fake breasts and fake nose," the ex said to Ali.

"Hey, watch your mouth," the boyfriend said. "The only fake person in this room is you."

"Screw you," the ex said.

"No, screw you."

My ex-wife picked up her wine glass and dumped it all over the boyfriend. That's my girl, I thought. She then picked up her purse and walk away from the table. This was turning out much better than I expected. I got up and ran after her.

"Hey, wait up," I said. "What the hell is the matter with you?"

"I can't stand him anymore," the ex said. "I hate my life."

"He seems like a real nice guy," I said.

"There is no such thing."

"Come on, he can't be any worse than me," I said.

"True."

"You sure know how to win a man's heart," I said.

"I miss you," my ex said.

I had a feeling that the ex's volcano of resentment towards me was cooling down, but that was totally unexpected. She said she missed me. My knees started to shake, and my heart was pounding so fast, I thought it was going to jump out of my chest. It felt just like the first time I saw her. I never thought I would hear those words again. But this was not a time for emotional hiccups or to be sentimental.

"Oh, you do? I thought I was the most horrifying person on the face of the earth. I'm not that bad after all, am I?"

"Yes, you are," she said.

"Okay, maybe you're right, and I recognize that, and that's a start, don't you think?"

"You're the most conniving, manipulative, devious person I've ever known, yet I desperately miss you," she said.

"That's part of my magic. What can I say?"

"Doesn't matter now. We each have gone our own separate ways," she said as she walked out of the restaurant.

I looked at Ali and the podiatrist. They were deep in a conversation and were paying no attention to me. Things were moving a lot faster than I had expected and I had a big decision to make: should I or shouldn't I? This was the most fragile I'd ever seen my ex, and it was my best chance to get her back, but at the same time, would that do me any good? If she got back with me, would life be any better than it was before? What guarantees did I have? Would the bickering start again, and would we both end up back where we were a few years ago?

Well, with all my mental deficiencies, I was smart enough to know that there are no guarantees in life. I might be a better person now than I was before, and the same might hold true for her. Or maybe we were both just a bit more bitter and unbearable. Or even worse, maybe we were just getting too good at concealing our intolerable personas. Who knows? Either way, this was a difficult decision and I had two seconds to make it.

"Wait," I yelled while running across the parking lot. "You're absolutely right."

"What?"

"You're right. I suck, and you, my dear, you suck, too."

"Excuse me?"

"Listen, let's cut the bullshit," I said. "We both know each other pretty well. As individuals we're both highly flawed, and that's okay. I have my faults, you have yours and we both are too old to change. But maybe, and just maybe, if each one us tries a little, and I mean just a little, to be a better person, we can live together without killing each other."

"I can be a better person," she said.

"Me, too, maybe. I don't know."

"What about Miss Perfect in there? Don't you like her?" she said.

"Who're you talking about?"

"Alison. What about her?"

"That's my buddy, Ali. He had a sex change operation. I planned the whole thing to get you back."

"Ali?"

"Yeah, he looks good, doesn't he?"

"No way."

"Yeah; a new set of wheels, a paint job, and there you have it: Alison."

"See? That's what I'm talking about. Everything is drama with you," she said.

"Hey, I did it for you."

"No, you did it for you," she said.

"No, I did it because I need to have you back in my life for the kids and for me. Can you just accept that?"

"Why do you want me back?"

"Good question," I said. "I hate your guts, hate your family, hate your nagging. Logically, I should be strangling you right now, but I'm crazy about you. I'm sick. Hey, what do you want me to say?"

The ex-wife got into her car and left me in the middle of the parking lot. I stood there like an idiot, wondering what had just happened. Did she leave on good terms or am I history? Did I overdo it? Was I too overly dramatic? Were the words coming out of my buttocks instead of my mouth? Can someone explain her behavior in simple terms? I wish I could understand women.

I walked back to the restaurant and joined Ali and the podiatrist. The two were getting pretty cozy in there. I felt like I was intruding.

"Sorry, I needed to have a little talk with her," I said.

"It's okay," the podiatrist said. "Alison told me everything."

"Everything?" I asked.

"Yes, and that's okay with me. Actually, I hope you don't take this personally, but the only people that can stand you two are probably yourselves," the boyfriend said.

"I don't know. I'm not sure where I stand at the moment," I said.

"It'll be okay," Ali said. "She'll come around."

"Oh, by the way," the boyfriend said, "if you don't mind, I'd like to spend some time with lovely Alison. We seem to have a lot in common."

"You sure she told you everything?" I asked the podiatrist.

"Yes. Sometimes you find your counterpart in the strangest circumstances."

The podiatrist grabbed Ali's hand and gently kissed it. I jumped out of my chair.

"Dude, this dude is a dude," I said.

"Yes, but he is my kind of a dude," The boyfriend said.

Okay, that was more than I needed to know. I was no longer needed in that place, and it was time for me to leave the lover boys by themselves. You can never get in the way of a good man finding a good man.

I was driving home when my cell phone rang. "Hi, I was wondering if you would like to come to dinner tomorrow night."

"Who? Me?"

"Yes, you," my ex said.

"Who all is coming?"

"You, and of course, the kids."

"What about your boyfriend?"

"He is not invited," she said.

"Can I bring Ali?"

"No, just you," she said.

"You sure? 'Cause Ali loves to hang with us like in the good old days."

"Stop it or I'll hang up."

"Okay, just kidding. What time?"

"Seven."

"I'm there."

I don't know how this will turn out. Grandpa used to say, "Marriage is like a big, fat watermelon: you never know what you're gonna get till you break it open and sink your teeth in it." Through years of living separate lives, the ex and I came to certain realizations. We both became conscious of the fact that marriage is like everything else in life: it is half planning and half dumb luck. It doesn't matter what you do, the moment you sign the dotted line, you are pretty much in hands of faith, with Mr. Murphy in the driver's seat. We also came to conclusion that in the game of life, you are sometimes a windshield and sometimes a bug. SPLAT! So we decided to stop taking ourselves too seriously; nobody else did.

I have no doubt that the wife and I will continue having our troubles, and there is no way for me to predict the future, but one thing I know for sure: I love my kids, I love my wife, and life is not complete without all of them with me under one roof. I'll probably continue to scam my way through life and give it my usual mediocre effort in everything I do, but at the end of the day, I'm a proud Iranican man who loves his roots, his adopted country, his family and friends and, most importantly, life itself. What else is there?

Printed in the United States
26114LVS00001B/243

9 781589 396777